A Bent Creek Wedding

Harker Brothers Ranch Book 3

Catie Cahill

Contents

Come Home to Bent Creek

A small town in Montana where everyone knows everyone, secrets live in the shadows of the mountains, and love is just waiting to be found. One by one, the Harker brothers return home to reclaim their ranch, face their family's past troubles with the Nobles, and find the love they didn't know they needed.

Chapter One

Ward

It was the school that almost made me turn around.

Carter Jones High School, still setting on the edge of town in all its 1950s gray cinderblock glory. It wasn't on my way to the address Gabe gave me on Custer Street, not even close. But my car found its way there anyway.

I pulled in a breath through my teeth as I rolled slowly past the school. It was late, almost sunset, and the place was empty. But I could swear that I still smelled the bleach and pencil-scented air inside and heard the squeak of shoes against the polished floors.

It made me smile for a minute, remembering my teenage self, more confident than any tall, gawky kid had the right to be. I wanted to rule student council and collect every classmate as a friend. And then it all crumbled around me, and no amount of practiced smiles or perfectly chosen words could undo the Harker family disaster.

The road wound downhill, and the town came into view.

Why was I here again?

I tapped my fingers on the steering wheel, thinking about how easy it would be to throw a U-turn right in the middle of this empty street and hightail it back to my apartment in Los Angeles. I wouldn't have to deal with this place, the people, or the past.

Except in LA, I'd have to face the fact that I was fired.

I pressed my foot to the gas and kept going. There was no way to avoid returning eventually, but if I was here, I could at least do what I came here for. And then I'd go back home with another win in my book. I needed that boost to my ego. It was the only way I'd find something that blew my old job at Luckett Enterprises out of the water.

Gabe's place was easy enough to find. In the middle of town and ridiculously picturesque. I lifted an eyebrow at the white lattice framing the porch as I shifted the car into park. It was a one-eighty from the sleek lines of the apartment complex I'd left behind in California. Marybeth Noble had made my stepbrother go small-town domestic.

It was June but the mountain air still had a bite to it. As I extracted my bag from the backseat, I tried not to think about how it smelled the exact same as it had years ago. Pine, earth, and, weirdly, something that reminded me of gravel. I couldn't pinpoint it, but it brought me right back to sitting on the front porch at the ranch, or stepping out back in the early morning dark to start the never-ending chores I shared with my brothers.

The porch steps creaked under my feet. A few flowerpots were scattered artfully around the porch, and hardy green plants poked up through the soil. It was all so perfect I half-expected to see a wreath or a big, cheerful *Welcome!* sign on the door. My ex-girlfriend Parker would've never gone for one of those signs. Or plants. She wasn't a fan of dirt.

Or you, I reminded myself as I raised a hand to knock on the door. Her rejection bit into the soft part of my mind. I ground my teeth as I shoved it away.

The door opened, and there stood my stepbrother. He looked nothing like the rest of us, with his dark blond hair and clear blue eyes. Parker thankfully forgotten, I stepped inside and embraced him.

"It's good to see you," Gabe said. He stood back and Nick was right behind him.

"Ward." Nick wrapped me in a bear hug before standing back and sizing me up. "What are you eating out there in California? Kale and avocados?"

"Mixed with quinoa," I said as I dropped my bag on the floor.

"Keen-what?" Nick shook his head before I could answer. "Didn't expect you to get here so early."

I eyed my oldest brother. We shared the same hair color and the same storm-colored eyes, but I'd have been laughed off the football field that Nick and Gabe had dominated in high school. "You bet I wouldn't show, didn't you?"

At least he had the decency to look sheepish.

"Pay up." Gabe held out his hand to Nick.

"I'm offended that you don't think I'm a man of my word." I couldn't keep the grin from my face. Needling Nick was something I'd missed. "Where's Jackson? Don't I deserve the entire welcoming party?"

"Work," Gabe replied as Nick slapped a fifty a little too hard against his hand. "He's doing construction up at the Summit Mountain Resort."

The ski resorts, keeping Bent Creek alive since forever. I was about to ask how he liked it when Marybeth Noble appeared in the doorway across the room. Her arms were folded gracefully against her chest. She smiled at me, but it was careful, as if she wasn't sure I'd be happy to see her here.

"Ward, you remember Marybeth?" Gabe's words were guarded, and I didn't miss the brotherly threat underlying his tone. *Be nice, even if she is a Noble.*

I didn't care about that. I never had. I gave Marybeth my most winning smile and lifted a hand. "How could I forget? You stole the Star Reader crown from me in third grade."

The corner of her mouth lifted in a genuine smile. "Move Forward with Ward," she said, quoting my sophomore year campaign slogan for class representative.

"Yeah. Unfortunately, everyone preferred Free Pizza with Justin." I made a face. "It didn't even rhyme."

"I don't think he ever delivered on that promise either," Marybeth said. Her arms were at her sides now. "I've got chili on the stove if you're hungry."

I glanced at Gabe, who was clearly relieved that I was cool with his girlfriend. "I get it now. She cooks."

He punched me in the arm and grabbed my bag from the floor. "Come on, I'll show you the room."

The house was small, and the second bedroom in the back was barely big enough to hold the furniture. It wasn't my too-expensive apartment with its exposed brick and minimalist feel, and it definitely wasn't one of the hotels I was used to when I traveled out of town for work, but something about it made the tension ease in my shoulders. I made quick work of unpacking and joined my brothers and Marybeth at the table in the dining room.

We kept the conversation light at first. Work, the town, stuff like that. I ribbed Nick about his second-time-around girlfriend, Larkin.

"You'll eat your words when we're married." He pointed at me with his fork.

"I thought you were backing off that for a while?" Marybeth fixed him with a frown. She and Larkin were inseparable in school, and I guessed that hadn't changed.

"I did," he said with a resigned sigh.

"She wants to marry you. She's more or less told me that. She just needs time," Marybeth replied.

"Or maybe she'll come to her senses," I teased, knowing that Larkin never would. I'd seen enough of the two of them together in high school to know that. They'd wind up in matching rocking chairs on the porch at eighty.

"Like Parker?" Nick didn't waste a second, hitting me right in the gut with that one.

I shoved a spoonful of chili into my mouth to bury the hurt that thinking of Parker always brought.

"That was low," Gabe said with a pointed look at our brother. It matched the one Marybeth gave him too.

I managed to shrug. "It wasn't serious." Never mind that I'd thought it was.

"Sorry, I shouldn't gone there." Nick eyed me now with that big brother concern.

I forced a smile. "It's fine. Better I saw who she really was before it went any further." Parker wanted me when I was on top of the world. When I fell off—even if it was just for a moment—she was done.

Nick exchanged a look with Gabe, and I knew they wanted to know what had happened. I hadn't told either one of them that I'd been sent packing from Luckett Enterprises. It wasn't something I really wanted to share with anyone, especially after it went so badly with Parker. "She was pissed I didn't want to buy a house. You know, one of those gated things with the long driveways?" I added a disbelieving chuckle at the end of my lie. It bordered on the truth, at least.

Nick's eyebrows dipped while Gabe tilted his head. It didn't matter that I hadn't seen them in years. They knew me too well—and they knew I wasn't being entirely honest. I dug my fingers into the napkin on my lap, willing them to leave well enough alone.

Gabe straightened, apparently deciding not to push it. "You dodged a bullet with that one. What if you married her?"

"Parker Harker." Nick laughed, and even Marybeth grinned.

It was enough to lighten the mood, and I laughed too. And it stayed that way till after dinner, when Gabe finally brought up the reason I was here.

"This isn't going to be easy, you know," he said after a lull in the conversation.

I didn't have to ask him what he was talking about. Instead, I leaned back in my chair, lifting the front legs from the floor, and let a lazy smile lift the corners of my mouth.

This I was good at.

"Bet you it will be. She hasn't met me yet." It felt good, letting that confidence wrap around me like a familiar old coat.

"She hasn't met us either," Nick said pointedly. "Pretty sure that's on purpose."

"Larkin said she's been coming in the coffee shop a few times a week since she's been staying in town," Marybeth said.

I let my gaze wander to her, wondering what she really thought of all this. But her expression betrayed nothing.

"You can trust her," Gabe said, like he was reading my thoughts.

"Never thought I couldn't." I grinned at Marybeth, and waited half a second before she smiled back. Out of all my brothers, I was the one who cared the least about the bad blood between our family and hers.

While Jackson and Nick had run headlong into fray, I tried to keep out of it, more like Gabe.

But unlike Gabe, I knew a lot more about where it came from. I wished I didn't, but when you're good at talking, people tend to spill their guts. Even your own Pops.

"The coffee shop's a good place to start," I said, a plan forming in my mind. Get her attention, win her trust, convince her that it was in her and her company's best interest to sell that land.

Easy.

"I'll ask Larkin what time she usually stops by," Nick said.

"Sounds good." I cracked my knuckles, ready to get started.

"She's a tough one," Gabe said, a note of warning lacing his voice.

I shrugged. I'd met my fair share of hard-nosed people—women and men. And I'd broken every one of them. "Nothing I can't handle."

Gabe nodded and then stood to help Marybeth clear the plates from the table. When they'd both disappeared into the kitchen, Nick leaned forward, resting his arms on the table.

"Did you go by there?" He didn't need to explain what he meant by *there*.

"No," I said curtly. "No need to."

He raised his eyebrows, like he didn't believe me.

"Look, I'll get her to sell the ranch to you. And then I'm gone. I've got a life back in California." *An apartment,* that voice in the back of my head reminded me. *That's all you've got.* No girlfriend, no job, no friends that ran any deeper than a few beers on a Saturday night. I shoved all that aside. "There's nothing for me here."

Nick frowned, and I realized I'd hit a nerve. They were here—him, Gabe, and Jackson. Three of my five brothers.

"My work is back in LA," I said carefully.

"Right." Nick gave a quick nod, like I hadn't just stuck a dagger in his gut and twisted it a little.

I drummed my fingers on the legs of the chair. I felt guilty, and I didn't like that. What did he expect, though? That I'd show up here, realize everything I'd been missing, and never leave again? Bent Creek was nothing but painful memories and secrets that would gnaw you from the inside out if you let them.

It was better to be somewhere else. *Anywhere* else.

"I don't know how you deal with it here," I said, the curiosity getting the better of me.

Looking at Nick was like looking in a mirror sometimes, and I fought the urge to turn away. "It's not what you think it is," he said quietly. "It's not what I thought it was when I came back here."

"What do you mean?" I hadn't stopped in town on purpose tonight. I figured I could deal with the stares and whispers tomorrow.

He shrugged. "This town is what you make of it."

"That's cryptic."

He laughed, just a little. "You'll see, if you give it a chance."

That wasn't going to happen. I didn't care about the Nobles or anything they'd supposedly done, not like my brothers cared, but I hadn't forgotten that they'd poisoned the entire town against us. And I'd kept up with my brothers' texts enough to know that Luke Noble was still hellbent on running them out of town.

But why they'd want to stay anyway was beyond my comprehension.

This place was steeped in memories of Pops, shady business, and secrets that were better off staying buried. I didn't want to revisit the person I'd been back then, struggling to find a place for myself through all of that. I didn't fit in here. I never had.

"I'm getting this done," I told Nick as I stood up. "And then I'm leaving."

Chapter Two

Violet

The buzz of the phone jerked my attention away from the list on my laptop.

Livvy. My sister's name moved slowly across the screen. I sighed loudly, slumped back as best I could into the rigid desk chair, and instantly regretted it as the wood bit into my spine. This bed and breakfast preferred aesthetics over function. I stared at Olivia's name. If she was calling instead of texting, it couldn't be good.

"Hey," I said, taking one last glance at my laptop screen before pushing it down to give my sister my full attention.

"Hey, Violet, hope I'm not bothering you." Her voice was a little breathless, as if she were chasing around her twin toddlers.

"Of course not." *Lie.*

No.

I squeezed my eyes closed and turned in the chair before opening them again. This was Livvy. The day I started thinking of her and my parents as a bother was the day I needed to seriously reexamine my priorities. "What's going on?"

Her sigh was heavy through the speaker. "You know the—Ellie! No, put that down!—Sorry. Trying to keep these kids alive takes every brain cell I have sometimes."

I couldn't help but smile. The twins, my nieces, had taken my heart the day they were born. "Tell them I'll bring them new stuffies if they listen."

"That is the *last* thing they need," Livvy said. But she repeated what I said, and the twins' squeals of delight pierced the distance through the phone. "Okay, where was I?"

"I don't think you'd even started." I pressed a hand against the top of the ornate desk and stood. I thought better when I walked, and I had a feeling that whatever Livvy was about to tell me was going to require some thinking.

"Okay, so do you remember how Dad's doctor mentioned that new medicine? The one that just got approved?"

"Yeah?" My heart thumped, and I crossed my fingers. The doctor had been really optimistic about that drug. She'd said it was keeping people from having to do another round of chemo.

"So she pulled some strings, and she was able to get him on the list for it."

I bit back my smile as I paced across the small, frilly room I had at the bed and breakfast. "But . . .?" I filled in for her, knowing there had to be a catch.

"It's a thousand dollars a month."

My stomach lurched. I pressed a hand against it and crossed to the window that overlooked a garden below. I took a deep breath in and slowly let it out as I focused on the pots of begonias and impatiens.

"Violet?" Livvy's voice was tentative through the phone.

I swallowed. "I heard you."

"Do you think we can do it?" There was a note of hope in her question.

I leaned my forehead against the window and closed my eyes. Everything with Dad's treatment was expensive, from the doctors' bills to the ramp we'd had installed at the house. I shouldn't have expected this to be any different.

"Yes," I heard myself say. "Of course we can."

"Okay, good. Okay." I could almost hear her nodding through the phone, one kid propped on her hip while she started scribbling down a to-do list. We worked well together, Livvy and I. She balanced everything at home—kept track of Dad's appointments and ran errands for Mom—while I paid the bills.

We talked a little longer before hanging up. I glanced at my laptop, knowing full well I should get back to work. Especially with a new thousand-dollar expense hanging over my head.

A thousand dollars a month. Instead of sitting at the desk, I pushed aside the lacy curtain and stared out the window again. How was I going to make that work? Something was going to have to give. Something big, like my apartment in Missoula.

I wasn't surprised, but it hurt all the same. It shouldn't matter, given how much I traveled for work. But the idea of moving back in with Mom and Dad not only made me feel like a failure, it meant there was no getting away—not even for a night—from the responsibilities I carried.

I needed a drink. But considering it was one o'clock in the afternoon and I still had hours of work ahead of me, coffee would have to do.

I threw on the neat top and perfectly fitting pants I had on earlier when I met with Chestnut Moon's real estate agent, Kyle Clemmons. Running a quick hand through my hair and tossing on a fresh coat of lipstick, I grabbed my purse and headed toward the coffee shop.

Luckily, no one was manning the front desk at the B&B when I crept down the stairs. The owners were friendly enough, but almost too friendly in that small-town way. I'd met a hundred people like them ever since I started working for Chestnut Moon and its associated companies. This one even came with a sweet old grandmother, a baby, and a tiny dog.

The front door creaked when I closed it behind me, and the floorboards on the porch echoed the sound. There was a weird sense of freedom when I put more than ten feet between myself and my laptop. It didn't make sense, considering that anyone could reach me on the phone in my purse, but still . . . it was nice to at least think I'd left work behind for a few minutes. More and more lately, I'd had to force myself to get the work done instead of letting myself get distracted.

As I strolled down the sidewalk toward Main Street, I could almost imagine I was someone else. A Violet who lived in a place like this, who had a job that didn't tie her stomach up in knots, whose family didn't rely on her paycheck to buy medicine and pay the bills. Maybe she'd have a dog and live in one of the cute little houses that lined the side streets in this town. She would probably be a regular at the coffee shop and go skiing up at one of the resorts a couple times a month. Her biggest worries would be what to make for dinner and whether her boyfriend would bring dessert.

The daydream was nice, and it kept work and Dad and giving up my apartment and the fact that I'd never had a real relationship out of my head for a few minutes. The sun was bright, people were out, and by the time I stepped into Mountain Roasters, I was in a much better mood than when I'd left the bed and breakfast.

The coffee shop was a cozy place—like the rest of Bent Creek—and it smelled of freshly roasted coffee beans. A few people were scattered at tables, some chatting, some working, and I smiled at the everydayness of it.

I stepped in line behind a woman with a long reddish-brown ponytail.

"Oh, sorry. I'm not waiting. Go ahead." She stepped aside, but her smile fell immediately when her eyes landed on my face.

My hand went immediately to my mouth, thinking I'd smudged my lipstick or completely missed something in my teeth from lunch.

Her smile returned, but it was tight and forced, almost as if she knew who I was and didn't like me at all.

"What can I get for you?" the woman behind the counter asked.

My gaze snapped to her. She was shorter, with dark hair and perfectly tan skin, but she wore the same not-really-a-smile as the other woman. I'd only been in here once, and I hadn't seen her then.

"Iced latte, please, with almond milk," I said in a perfectly pleasant voice.

"We're out of almond milk," the barista replied, her words curt but not rude.

"How about oat milk?"

She gave a quick nod and got to work. I could feel the other woman's eyes on me. I forced a glance at her.

"So, how long are you in town for?" she asked, and that's when I realized she was wearing a shirt with a Christmas tree on it. In June.

"I'm not sure yet," I said carefully. *Why do you want to know?* The question was burning a hole through my tongue as I kept it silent. Bent Creek was a small town, so it wasn't surprising that they'd pegged me as an outsider. I also wouldn't be surprised if they already knew who I was.

"Hmm," was all she said in return.

"I'm Violet Barnes." I extended a hand, practically oozing professionalism but secretly hoping she'd return the favor and satisfy my raging curiosity.

"Marybeth Noble." She hesitated half a second before shaking my hand. The name meant nothing to me, but the hesitation did. And that's when it hit me. It wasn't me they disliked—it was the company I represented. I'd have to dig through my files when I got back to my laptop. See if the name Noble popped up anywhere.

The woman behind the counter set my drink down. "It's four thirty-five. Is this on you or Chestnut Moon?" She said the name of the company with barely disguised distaste, confirming exactly what I'd thought. I skimmed her nametag before opening my purse. *Larkin.* The first name alone meant nothing either.

"Just me," I said, tapping my card against the reader before dropping a dollar into the tip jar despite the frosty service.

They both watched me as I returned my card to my purse. I picked up my coffee and raised it. "Have a good day!"

I couldn't get out of there fast enough, but I forced myself to walk normally. Those two had single-handedly dashed my daydream of uprooting my entire life and living in this town. I'd never be welcome here, for reasons I didn't entirely understand.

Chestnut Moon was in the business of buying property and selling to developers. Most of the transactions I'd facilitated were easy. People who sold were usually eager to get the money. There were a few who needed more convincing, and then a handful that had been outright hostile. But I was particularly good at the latter, soothing anger and convincing people that selling was in their best interests. It worked every time, even if it sometimes left me feeling a little guilty.

I sipped the latte as I walked slowly back to the bed and breakfast. I smiled at a few people I walked by, and they smiled back. Not everyone hated me and my company. A couple of people in little towns north of here felt like we hadn't paid them enough, sure. If anyone asked them what they thought of Chestnut Moon or Willow Cosmos or whatever LLC we'd used to buy the property, they'd probably have a few choice words about the company, and me as its representative.

But here, in Bent Creek . . . I mentally paged through every sale I'd facilitated since I'd been assigned here last year when the company took a stronger interest in buying land in this area. None of them were particularly difficult; no one had been angry. In fact, the only thing that had been out of the ordinary was having to get the police to remove a couple of squatters in one of the properties we owned. But those were Harkers—the family that had owned the land years ago—not . . .

My latte sloshed in its cup as I stopped suddenly on the sidewalk.

The woman I'd shaken hands with had introduced herself as Marybeth Noble. *Noble*. I could be misremembering, but I was pretty sure that was the name of the guy who'd asked me out to dinner once a few months ago, and then casually let me know about the squatters on that old ranch property.

Luke Noble. That was it. I ran the name over and over again in my head as I turned off Main Street. He was cute enough, with that hair that curled slightly at the ends, tall and muscular with that cowboy thing going on. He didn't make my heart skip a beat or anything, but he'd been nice enough when he asked me out. Considering I hadn't gone out with anyone in at least a year, I'd said yes and actually enjoyed myself. I never heard from him again after the squatter tip-off.

But none of that made any sense with the way Marybeth Noble eyed me like I was her sworn enemy. Unless . . . My eyes widened, and I felt a little sick to my stomach. Was she his *wife*? Hopefully ex-wife. Maybe it was personal, and had nothing to do with Chestnut Moon.

That had to be it, because nothing else made sense. If I saw her again, I'd explain what happened.

I was so lost in thought that as I climbed the steps to the B&B's porch, I didn't even notice the man waiting for me until he rose from the rocking chair and stepped right in front of me.

Chapter Three

Ward

She was prettier than her picture.

That was my first thought. My second thought was about how easy this was going to be.

She didn't appear to notice me at all as I rose from the rocking chair and crossed the porch to cut her off.

"Oh!" She squeaked in surprise, fingers crushing the plastic cup in her hand. "I'm sorry, I didn't see you there."

"That's interesting. I'm usually hard to miss." I let my eyes take their time examining her from top to bottom. It was a tactic, designed to demonstrate superiority and to make the other person uncomfortable. But I sure didn't mind using it now.

Violet Barnes was a heck of a lot nicer to look at than most of the old men I had to take down a peg or two back in LA. Her light brown hair barely skimmed the bottom of her pointed chin. She wore a fitted white button-up top and pants that screamed no-nonsense, but her heels were higher than was practical. They looked like the kind of thing most women would wear out to a club or to a date with someone they wanted to impress.

The thought that she was more than all-business made the corners of my lips turn up.

"Are you looking for something?" Instead of crossing her arms defensively, like a lot of people did, she stood taller and raised that little chin at me.

That only made my smile grow broader. Okay, maybe this wouldn't be easy, but this one was going to be fun.

"Not in particular. Ward Harker." I stuck out my hand.

Violet didn't miss a beat. Her hand was slim, her nails were perfectly manicured, and she shook my hand with a grip that half the men I'd met couldn't match.

"Harker," she repeated, not bothering to introduce herself. She knew that I already knew who she was, and I liked that she didn't mess around with pretending she didn't.

"You've heard of us." I leaned against the doorframe, like this was some casual conversation.

"Us?" She arched a delicate eyebrow. "How many of you are there?"

I laughed at that. She was better off not knowing. "I have a few brothers. But I'm the only one you need to know right now."

The corner of her mouth rose in amusement. She liked me. Score one for Ward Harker.

"Were you the one I had put in jail?" She sipped the frothy concoction in her Mountain Roasters cup while she eyed me in the most innocent way possible.

I decided I liked her too. "Jail doesn't agree with me. I have higher standards for my accommodations."

"Mmm," she said, nodding. "Must've been one of those brothers you mentioned."

I ran a hand across my chin, letting my eyes dart away as if I was only half-interested in what she had to say. "So how long are you in town for?"

"Is that a line?"

I dragged a lazy gaze back to her and raised my own eyebrow this time. "What do you think?"

She studied me a moment, her pink lips closing around that straw again. I had to force my eyes away. I knew better than to fall for the oldest trick in the book, even though I could've stood there all day, watching her drink that coffee.

"I think you want something from me, Mr. Harker," she finally said.

"And what would that be, Miss Barnes? Or is it Mrs. Barnes?" There was no ring on her finger. I'd already looked.

She ignored the second question, keeping those brown eyes on me. "I don't know, but it's big enough that you'd come wait out here on this porch for me."

I pushed myself away from the doorframe, standing taller and closing the few inches between us. Violet didn't move a muscle. "Maybe I was looking for conversation. Maybe I was just out here, enjoying the fresh air."

She dropped the coffee cup to her side. "I've got work to do. Ask your question."

Now we were getting somewhere. "What kind of work? Snatching up a few more properties outside of town?"

There was only the slightest twitch of a muscle over her eyebrow at that. It was impressive, how much she was able to keep off her face.

"I do work for a real estate investment company." She narrowed her eyes slightly and tilted her head. "Do you have something to sell? Or are you fishing around for a lead on where you might crash tonight?

I don't really need to find another one of you living in one of our properties."

I laughed and shoved my hands into my pockets. She was on the verge of underestimating me, and maybe that was what I needed in this situation. So I fixed her with a friendly grin, and said, "I'm more interested in buying."

She shrugged. "Can't help you with that. We don't have anything for sale. Now if you'll—" She stepped to the side, ready to end the conversation.

I moved in the same direction, blocking her entrance with my arm across the door and my hand pressed against the frame on the opposite side.

A hint of annoyance crossed her face, the first indication I'd seen of any real emotion beyond amusement breaking through. I could use that. In fact, I could turn it into something else.

"Do you have another question?" She gave me a pointed look.

I let the laziest of smiles float across my face as I kept my eyes on her. "What if I said I was looking for a place to crash? You got an extra couch up in your room?"

The muscles around her lips tightened, and as good as I was at reading people, I couldn't tell if she was holding back a laugh or a stream of curse words.

But then she rose up on her toes and leaned forward until her mouth was right next to my ear. "No," she whispered, her breath tickling my neck and bringing goose bumps to my arms. "But I'm sure you can find some gullible woman to take you in. Or maybe an empty house to break into."

Then she leaned back on her heels, ducked under my arm, and disappeared into the bed and breakfast.

Slowly, I dropped my arm and turned around. She'd left the door open, but there was no sign of her inside. Only Suzanne Dowling, who Gabe told me ran the place now with her grandmother.

"Ward? Is that you?" Suzanne's voice carried across the entryway.

I raised a hand in greeting. Suzanne was a couple of years older than me. She'd been in class with Gabe and Nick, a pretty cheerleader that half the guys in school had a crush on.

"I saw Nick up at Town Square Hardware yesterday, and he mentioned you were back in town." Suzanne leaned a hand on the desk and gestured to me with her other hand. "Come in! Do you need a place to stay? We have rooms available."

The Dowlings were just as desperate for business as every other place in Bent Creek. Gabe had hinted at Marybeth's woes with her Christmas shop, and while there were people out on Main Street, it wasn't nearly as many as I remembered seeing as a kid.

"I'm good," I said, taking a step inside. "I'm staying with—" A door shut somewhere upstairs, and a wild idea took root in my mind. "You know what? Put me down for a room, something upstairs." I yanked my wallet from my pocket before I could change my mind. This was both dangerous and brilliant.

"Really?" Suzanne clapped her hands together, making me think she was going to erupt into a cheer right then and there.

"Sure. I like this place." I handed her a credit card.

A smile exploded across Suzanne's face. "Gran and I put a lot of work into it. I'll give you Room Three. The Cedar Room. It's one of my favorites."

"Great," I said as I glanced up the stairs. Violet Barnes wasn't going to know what hit her when I turned up at breakfast in the morning.

Before the week was out, she was going to sell me the ranch property. She just didn't know it yet.

Chapter Four

Violet

I debated tearing open a granola bar before getting to work, but one glance at my laptop had me wanting to run the other way.

I stared at it a moment, wondering when I'd gone from loving what I did to dreading it. I chalked it up to the stress with Dad and left to go downstairs to the dining room. Suzanne and her grandmother made an incredible breakfast, and my stomach rumbled just thinking about it.

"Good morning, Violet! I'll get you some coffee," Suzanne said from the door to the kitchen. Her baby babbled from behind her, and the little dog she'd gotten for her grandmother yipped. It reminded me so much of Livvy's house that I couldn't help but smile.

"Thanks," I said before glancing down at the short menu laying on the lacy placemat in front of me. I ran my fingers over the lace as I studied it. Eggs and bacon, French toast, or—

"I hope they have huckleberry pancakes. There's nothing like homemade huckleberry pancakes."

I recognized that voice. Heart simultaneously sinking and fluttering like a hyper butterfly, I looked up.

Ward Harker sat sprawled out in the chair across from me. He ran a hand through neat dark hair that fell right back into place before picking up the menu. "Hmm. No huckleberry pancakes. That's awfully disappointing."

"Huckleberries aren't in season." It was all I could think of to say. If he meant to catch me off-guard by showing up for breakfast at the B&B, he'd succeeded.

"I bet Mrs. Dowling makes a mean French toast," he said, eyes fixed on the menu. He looked so out of place in this dainty room, it was almost ridiculous. Dowling Bed & Breakfast was made for honeymooning couples and older women on weekend getaways. Not men like Ward Harker—tall, dark, and probably had a record a mile long, if the rumors I'd heard about his family were true.

He looked up and smiled at me then, almost as if he knew what I was thinking.

That wouldn't do. I leaned forward, resting my hands on the table. I was just about to cut Ward down another notch when Suzanne appeared, baby in one arm and coffeepot in her free hand.

"Coffee, Ward?" she asked as she poured some into my cup.

The baby stared at me as Ward nodded. "Sounds good. That little one sure is cute."

She beamed and dropped a kiss on the baby girl's head. "Thanks. Her name is Annie."

"Well, Annie, it looks like you're going to grow up to be just as smart and pretty as your mama," Ward said in a voice so smooth that a pink flush rose to Suzanne's cheeks.

"You're too sweet," Suzanne said as I silently gagged. I knew Ward's type. I'd met a hundred versions of him. Every word out of his mouth had an ulterior motive. He was either trying to get into Suzanne's pants or angling for a free breakfast. Or he was trying to make me jealous, which was so unbelievable a thought that I almost laughed.

"How'd you sleep? I always worry about those front rooms with the streetlights," she went on to ask Ward.

He *stayed* here last night? I had to fight to school my expression as my hand curled around the handle of my coffee mug.

"Just fine. Like a baby." He reached out a hand toward the actual baby, who gripped one of his fingers.

"Oh, good. Do you know what you want to eat?" Suzanne smiled at both of us. If she had any questions about why in the world Ward Harker was sitting with me, she kept them to herself. But if I knew small towns, I had a feeling word about our breakfast rendezvous would make it to every single person who lived in Bent Creek before noon.

"Ladies first." Ward inclined his head toward me.

I resisted the urge to shoot him a scowl and instead smiled back at Suzanne. "Eggs and bacon, please."

Suzanne nodded and turned to Ward, who ordered the French toast. And as soon as Suzanne had left to attend to the only other guests in the room, he leaned back in his chair and grinned at me.

"I'd pegged you for a yogurt and fruit girl," he said.

I wanted to swat that smug look right off his impossibly handsome face. Instead, I clasped my hands on the table and got straight to the point. "Why are you here?"

He leaned forward, face drawn into a serious expression. "Well, you see, my parents loved each other very much, and they'd decided that two boys weren't enough, so—"

"*At* this table," I said a little too loudly. "Staying at this B&B."

He shrugged. "I'm hungry, I needed a place to stay, and it's better to eat with company, don't you think?"

"Depends on the company."

"You're in luck, then. I'm downright pleasant to share a meal with." That sexy smile spread across his face and lit up his eyes, and all I could think about was whether he still smelled like woodsmoke and soap, the way he did last night when I leaned forward to whisper in his ear.

Which was *exactly* what he wanted. *Get it together, Violet.*

"I prefer eating with people who haven't committed felonies." I leaned back into my own chair, my eyes never leaving his.

Ward arched an eyebrow. "You're mistaking me for my brothers. A criminal record wouldn't have been conducive to my plans."

I tapped a nail against the screen of my phone, which lay on the table. "So if I Googled you right now, not a single arrest would show up?"

He lifted both hands. "Squeaky clean."

"Hmm." I didn't even know how many of them there were, much less who was who. The Harkers had only held my interest for as long as it took to get one of them out of the ranch house he'd broken into with his girlfriend.

So the fact I was suddenly dying to pick up my phone and do exactly what I'd suggested made no sense at all.

"My company still has nothing for sale," I said, drawing my hands together again and forcing myself not to type *Ward Harker* into a Google search.

"Right now." He eyed me as if he was calculating exactly what it might take for me to offer him his choice of properties.

"Ever."

"So you, what—buy up property and then do nothing with it? I find that hard to believe. Especially with how much your company has purchased around here lately." The glint in his gray-blue eyes had shifted from flirtatious to something harder, more determined.

"We're a real estate investment company. That means we buy when it's right and sell when it's right."

"What if I told you that now is the right time to sell?"

I laughed. "You couldn't afford it."

He leaned forward then, his gaze intent on me. I fought the urge to swallow. "How would you know that? You admitted to not knowing me from my brothers, much less anything else about me. And I haven't even told you which property I'd want to buy."

"I'm pretty sure I know which one." I spoke quickly to keep my voice even. I hated that this guy was having any kind of effect on me at all. It was taking everything I had to keep an impassive look on my face.

"You do," he said evenly. "And you're going to sell it to me."

"And what makes you think I'd ever do that?" Not that I even had the power to. Everything I did was dictated by the company's board, as distasteful as it sometimes was.

His eyes softened and the corner of his mouth rose again. "I can be very persuasive."

A hundred different images flew through my mind with those words. I dropped my hands to my lap and dug them into the cloth napkin to ground myself. Then I pressed my lips together and lifted my chin just slightly. "You can quit flirting with me. It won't work."

"But you can flirt with me? How is that fair?"

"I *didn't* flirt with you."

He jerked his head toward the front door. "Um, last night. Remember?"

Oh, right. "That wasn't flirting."

Ward laughed. "Sure it wasn't."

I dug my fingers into the napkin. "That was me, telling you in no uncertain terms that I wasn't interested. Because *you* were flirting with *me*."

"You were hardly an inch from my face. All hot breath and whispered words. I don't know how they do it in Missoula, but that sure felt like flirting to me."

I threw my napkin on the table, not missing the fact that he somehow knew where I'd grown up. "Look, Harker. I'm here for work. Nothing else. And even if I was, it wouldn't be with the likes of you."

"I beg to differ. I'm just your type."

I stood, past ready to be done with this conversation. "I'm not interested in criminals—for personal or business purposes."

He looked up at me, that obscenely devilish smile growing even broader. "You keep saying that. The worst thing I ever did was bend a few laws in the name of getting things done. If you'd looked me up on the internet like you said you wanted to, you'd know that."

"I'm not wasting my time on you. I have work to get done." And with that, I stalked out, back to the stairs and up to my room—with no breakfast, and the sneaking suspicion that Ward Harker had almost certainly done his own share of internet stalking.

About me.

Chapter Five

Marybeth

"You want me to do what now?" Gabe eyed the stack of old Christmas cards like they were going to jump up and shower him in Santa hats and stocking stuffers while singing "Jingle Bells" at full volume.

"It's easy, I promise. You cut out a piece of the card. Hole punch at the top. Thread a ribbon through. Tie the ribbon. And *voila*!" I demonstrated with a flourish.

"Okay." He sat down and dropped his hat on the table. It made me smile, seeing him wearing it all the time now. When he first came back to town last Christmas, he'd been dressed in a suit and looking nothing like the Gabe I'd crushed on so hard in high school. But now he was back to doing what he loved, ranch work, and I'd never get tired of him wearing a cowboy hat.

I handed him a pair of scissors and one of the cards I'd scored for pennies at the flea market.

"So . . ." he said as he picked up the scissors. "Why exactly?"

"Why what?" I was already stringing a length of red ribbon through another cut-out.

"Are you hanging these on a tree or something?" He gestured at the cards.

I paused. "Oh, that's an idea! But no, these are going to hang from the ceiling. Bent Creek Christmas needs a little decorating update." A *cheap* decorating update. Sales had been picking up a little since I'd started carrying non-Christmas items. Seasonal things, like Easter baskets, swim goggles, and St. Patrick's décor brought in people I hadn't seen in the store since Christmas. And it turned out that the tourists doing summer vacations at the resorts really liked buying sunblock, sunglasses, koozies, and other things they hadn't realized they'd needed for a whitewater rafting adventure or a hike. It wasn't much, but it was a start, and I felt better about the business than I had in months.

"What about—oops." Gabe held up two pieces of a square. He'd cut off a snowman's head.

"You have a warped sense of humor," I said, pointing my scissors at him.

"It was an accident, I swear." But he smiled as he picked up another card, and I couldn't help but laugh.

"Never mind. I'll get Larkin and Emily to help instead."

"Am I that bad?"

"You're decapitating snowmen, so yes."

He was out of his seat and by my side in seconds. "Then how about we do something else. Take advantage of all this summertime daylight." He tugged on my arm.

I sighed, as if I really preferred cutting out Christmas cards to spending time with him, and slowly rose from my chair. Gabe wrapped his arms around me and looked down.

"You're cute when you're annoyed," he said.

I wrinkled my nose at him. "What did you have in mind?"

"Not much. Maybe wandering by the hardware store and pricing out what we need to build a chicken coop."

I squealed and gripped his arms as I jumped up and down in my seat like a five-year-old. "Really? Tonight?"

"We finally have the time, so why not? I know how much you miss those Christmas chickens."

A little stab pinched my heart. I missed my flock *so* much. I'd given them all Christmas names and taken care of them like they were my children—up until a few months ago, when my brother basically told me never to come back to the ranch.

I chewed on my lip, thinking for a minute.

"What's wrong?" Gabe asked, his forehead creasing in worry.

"What if Luke won't give them to me? They really belong to the ranch. Not me."

"He'll give them to you if I have anything to say about it." Gabe's arms tightened around me as I glanced up at him. I appreciated his protective instinct, more than he'd ever know. But the last thing I wanted was a confrontation between him and my brother, especially when we'd all been living in an uneasy peace lately.

Of course, that peace meant Luke acted like I didn't exist and Gabe and Jackson had to rein in Nick every time Luke so much as crossed the street a block away. I hated it, but I didn't know how to change it, and it was better than the alternative.

"You're not going to do anything about it." I tapped him on the chest. "I'll get new chickens if I have to." But I *really* didn't want to. I wanted my girls. I hoped Luke would understand.

If he gave me the opportunity to even ask.

Gabe eyed me for another second before dropping a kiss to my forehead and grabbing his hat. "All right, get your jacket."

I slid my arms into the sleeves, grateful for the warmth the moment we stepped outside. It might have felt like summer during the day, but the moment the sun began to sink behind the mountains, summer became a distant memory.

I reached for Gabe's hand, and we strolled down the sidewalk, dodging kids' bikes, stopping to pet a neighborhood cat, and waving to Mrs. Foley, Emily's mom, from across the street.

A few people were out on Main Street, most of them making their way to or from one of the restaurants or bars. We stepped into Town Square Hardware twenty minutes before it closed, and spent every second of that time adding up the cost of plywood, chicken wire, nails, and anything else we could think of. After another solid ten minutes of conversation with old Mr. Lewis, we stepped outside as he locked the door behind us.

"It's not as bad as I thought," Gabe said, studying the note he'd created on his phone. "I can start on it this weekend, and finish it on my paycheck next week."

"I'll pay for it," I said quickly, not wanting Gabe to ever feel like I was mooching off him.

"I've got it," he said, shoving the phone into his pocket. And then, almost as if he could sense what I was about to say, he held his hand up. "No arguing. Let me do this for you. You just see about getting those chickens."

"Thank you," I said, snuggling under his arm as we walked.

I was soaking up all of Gabe's warmth and trying to figure out if it was better to approach Luke through a text or a phone call when Gabe stopped at the town hall.

"Suddenly interested in local politics?" I joked as he perused the monthly town council meeting agenda posted under the plexiglass on the outside wall.

He made a face. "No, but this caught my attention."

I squinted at the words under his finger. Sandwiched between *Summer Carnival Plans* and *Mowing Ordinance* were the words *Development Proposal & Eminent Domain Action.*

"Eminent domain," I read out loud. "Isn't that where the town or state or whatever takes your land?"

"They force you to sell. I think it needs to have a public benefit, like building a road." Gabe rubbed his hand over my arm as we walked on. "I wonder what it's for. And what they want to buy."

A sick feeling curled up my throat. It had only been six months since that real estate firm Gabe worked for in Chicago had tried their darnedest to get me to sell them the building that housed Bent Creek Christmas.

"It's not your shop," Gabe said, reading my mind. "You'd know about it before it landed on the town council agenda, right?"

"Right." It made sense. I'd have already gotten a letter or been approached. "It's weird that no one else has said anything, though."

Bent Creek was way too small for something like that to stay a secret.

Chapter Six

Violet

"But you're feeling better?" I tapped the toe of my canvas shoe against a landscape stone in the B&B's back garden.

"A lot better," Dad said with so much conviction that I almost believed him. But I knew better by now. For Dad, "feeling better" really just meant he could get out of bed and maybe go to the couch or the kitchen table. Even with a barrage of meds, the pain was always there. "Ready to take up bowling again."

"That's good," I said with a laugh as I remembered all those evenings spent in the bowling alley when I was a kid. "I'll tell Mom to let the league know."

Dad coughed and I stared hard at some kind of lily blooming in the garden. It was a gorgeous day—sunshine, white puffy clouds, warm. When I went out for a run earlier, I couldn't stop staring at the way the mountains looked like something off of a travel website. I'd always thought that about the mountains at home, and to have the same feeling here was . . . weird. Almost like I'd never left Missoula.

I moved slowly down the path as Dad put Mom back on the phone, and she told me about the new medicine and how much she thought it was going to help him. "Thank you," she said, quietly, probably so Dad couldn't hear. "We couldn't have done it without you."

"You don't have to thank me." I perched on the edge of a stone bench under an archway covered in vines. "I'm just glad I can *do* something."

Mom was quiet then, and I knew exactly what she was thinking. There wasn't a lot we could do, any of us. Dad's cancer would either slow down and go into remission, or it wouldn't. Even if I could buy all the medicine in the world, it might not save him.

"Oh, Livvy's here," she said. "She's coming with the girls to sit with your dad while I run some errands."

I smiled at the image of my rambunctious nieces spilling into Mom and Dad's small house. I'd empty my bank account over and over again to give Dad more time with his grandkids—and us. I'd be broke, move into their spare bedroom, and sell everything I owned to buy a few more years.

Which reminded me that I still needed to give notice on my apartment lease by the end of the month.

"Okay, I'll let you know when I figure out a day to move stuff in. And don't let Dad get too tired with the kids. Tell him I worry about him."

We said goodbye, and I held my phone in my lap as I stared out into the garden.

"You moving?" a male voice said from next to me. Before I knew it, Ward Harker had settled himself onto the bench right next to me. The bench was tiny, barely enough room for two kids, never mind two adults. His leg and arm pressed right up against mine.

I stood quickly before I could give too much thought to how warm he was. "What are you talking about?"

"Your phone call." He nodded at my phone before leaning back on the bench with both hands, taking up all the space where I used to be.

"Were you eavesdropping?" I shoved my phone into my pocket, wondering exactly how much he'd heard.

"You can't exactly call it that when you're having a conversation in a public place. It's a nice day. I was taking a walk." He stretched out his legs, leaning a foot against my ankle.

I stepped sideways. "Yeah, moving. So what? People move all the time." I cringed inwardly at how defensive I sounded.

"What about your dad? Is he okay?"

My blood froze. The *last* thing I was talking about with this guy was my father's health situation. "He's fine."

"Really? It didn't sound that way from your conversation. I hope he isn't very sick." He paused for a half a second, as if he was deciding whether or not to say more. "My stepmom was sick a lot before we lost her. Cancer."

I stared at him. He blinked, nonplussed, and I couldn't see what was behind those gray-blue eyes. He couldn't *know* about Dad, could he? Then again, he knew where I was from, so it was entirely possible.

Except it didn't seem like he was using it as ammunition against me. Instead . . . it sounded like he actually cared.

I opened my mouth, ready to say something that would open me up, make me vulnerable, and then I wrenched it shut again. I didn't tell anyone about Dad. I'd been with my last boyfriend when Dad was diagnosed, and I hadn't told him a thing. I pretended everything was okay.

Some things were just better kept private.

Plus, I'd done exactly what Ward had said to do—I'd Googled him. I didn't find a record, but his professional life was criminal enough. He was a snake, slithering through companies and striking where he found a weakness. Mergers that never should have happened went through, and acquisitions that should have died on a boardroom table magically occurred. And behind them all was Ward Harker.

Now here he was, doing the exact same thing to me. Weaving his way in, looking for a soft spot so he could bite.

I pushed my shoulders back and popped a hand onto my hip. He wouldn't find anything weak with me. I was a fortress, built to withstand attacks from sellers' attorneys, angry landowners, and dark-haired men with gazes that could melt the strongest of women.

"You're wasting your time. I'm not selling that property to you. Ever."

That got his attention. He stood, slowly brushing off the black top he wore, the one I wished I hadn't noticed clung to every line of muscle on his chest and arms. "I didn't ever say which one I wanted."

"I don't have time for games. You want the ranch land that used to belong to your family."

He ran a hand over his chin, eyeing me. "All right. If we're being direct, how much do you want for it?"

"It's not for sale."

"Come on. Everything's for sale. Why buy all those properties if you don't want to turn a profit?"

"Not my decision to make."

"You're underestimating yourself. I imagine you have more power than you think you do." He took a step forward, and I had to look up to see him.

I *hated* looking up. It was better to be on even ground, not feeling small. But I also refused to step back. I wasn't giving an inch of space up to this man.

"I don't underestimate anything. It's not mine to sell, and even if it was, I wouldn't sell it to you."

He kept that gaze on me. "There it is. You don't like me."

"I didn't say that." He drove me crazy, showing up and cornering me all the time. And I didn't like the way he operated in his career. But truth be told, I didn't know him well enough to say I didn't like him.

His eyes glinted blue in the sunlight that filtered through the arch and a nearby tree. It was weirdly intriguing, the way they could shift between blue and gray depending on the light. "So you *do* like me."

I crossed my arms. "You couldn't convince me with logic, so now you're back to flirting."

He raised his hands, devilish grin back right where he'd left it. "I didn't say it, you did."

"What are you talking about? I didn't say anything."

"By saying nothing, you said everything."

I blinked at him, completely lost. And then, out of nowhere, he lifted a hand and used his thumb to brush my cheek.

I jerked backward, my hand going immediately to my face. "What are you doing?"

"You had a speck of pollen." He gestured at his own cheek.

"Right." My face burned, but nowhere was it as hot as the skin he'd grazed under his fingertip.

And as if my heart wasn't pounding hard enough, my phone vibrated in my pocket, almost making me jump. I yanked it out, glad to have something to do other than looking at Ward's smirking expression and sharply angled jaw.

I barely registered the name on the screen before I answered it. "Violet Barnes." My voice was smooth and professional despite the marching band thumping inside my body.

"Barnes." Mac Russell's no-nonsense voice blared through the speaker.

I pulled the phone away from my ear just slightly. Ward didn't step back or do anything to indicate he was giving me privacy to take this call.

It figured.

"What's going on?" I asked, turning away from Ward.

"We have a problem," he said.

I dug my fingers into my palm as I focused on the decorative grasses waving in the breeze nearby. I really hoped that problem wasn't Ward Harker. If he'd truly been standing here, fake-flirting with me while in the background he'd done something to mess with Chestnut Moon or our investments, I swore—

"Eminent domain. You ever heard of it?"

I wrinkled my forehead. That wasn't where I expected this to go. "Sure, I know a little about it."

"Well, get ready, because you're going to become an expert. Some small-town, backwater investor thinks it's a great idea to convince the county to seize one of our properties. I don't know what they want to build. Something called—" The sound of papers rustling echoed through the speaker. "Thrill Mountain. What the hell is a Thrill Mountain?"

"I don't know," I said, but Mac wasn't waiting for my thoughts.

"I want you at this town meeting on Thursday. Seven o'clock. Don't say anything, just get a feel for the room. See if you can find out who's behind this. I'll scan the offers they sent over to you. Call Julia if you have questions."

And with that, Mac hung up, already talking to someone else before the line went dead.

"Eminent domain, huh? Sounds very . . . legal."

I should've known Ward would've heard every word. Mac wasn't exactly quiet. "I need to get back to work."

Ward inclined his head. "Don't let me keep you."

I paused mid-step. "What, you aren't going to spend another hour trying to convince me to sell to you? Or brushing my hair out of my face or something?"

He shrugged, as if it meant nothing to him at all. "I can if you want me to. I'm pretty good with the whole brushing hair from your face thing."

My face heated at the very thought. What was wrong with me? "I'm good, thanks," I said in my most sarcastic voice.

That only made his smile grow. "All right. Let me know if you change your mind. Otherwise, I'll see you at breakfast—if not before."

And then he sauntered away, leaving me steaming mad and completely confused, alone in the garden.

Chapter Seven

Ward

I was cracking Violet Barnes's shell, bit by bit. The only problem was that she'd somehow worked her way into half the thoughts I had throughout the day—and not all of them were business-related.

I'd made a big mistake, touching her face like that. I did it on a whim, thinking it would soften her toward me. It might've worked, except I kept reliving the moment, over and over again. How soft her skin was, how warm it felt against my thumb, the way she pulled in a delicate gasp when I made contact with her cheekbone.

I ran my hands over my face. That was enough. I had to quit thinking of her like that. If I went down that path, I'd ruin everything. Flirting was fine, but anything that made me feel like I was about to cross a line into feeling something was not. Even if she wasn't holding on to my family's legacy with tight purse strings, I had no business getting involved with someone so soon after Parker ditched me.

Because despite the image I portrayed, I was no good at flings. *Serial monogamist*, one of my old friends at Luckett Enterprises always said, shaking his head like it was a pity I couldn't run through women the way he did.

I had to get close to Violet and keep my distance, all at the same time.

I let out a frustrated sigh as I knocked on Nick and Jackson's door. Jackson answered, his girlfriend Emily right behind him. I didn't know what I was doing here—looking for advice, maybe. Or just not wanting to be alone.

"Hey," my brother said, pulling the door open wider. "What's wrong?"

I forced a smile, realizing I'd probably been grimacing when he'd opened the door. "Nothing. Maybe something. I don't know yet. Hey, Emily."

"Hey," she said, glancing between me and Jackson and probably trying to figure out if we needed some privacy. I'd only seen her a couple of times since I've been back in town, but she seemed to be a nice enough girl. Way better than I ever thought Jackson could wrangle. "Why don't I get you something to drink?"

"I'm good, but thanks," I said.

"All right." She stood on her tiptoes and kissed Jackson on his cheek. "I'll keep an eye on your sauce."

"You cooking?" I asked my brother as Emily disappeared into the kitchen.

"Yeah." He rubbed a hand across the back of his neck. "Never thought I'd be so into it, but I always kind of liked it, so it makes sense, right?"

"Sure. I can't make toast without burning it, so it's probably better than I could do."

"Sit." Jackson pointed at the sagging couch. "Talk."

I sat, while he put himself in a nearby chair. "Have you heard from Colt or Maverick lately?" I was stalling, asking him if he'd heard from our younger brothers.

He shrugged. "A week or two ago, maybe. Not sure where Colt is. I don't think he stays in one place long. Mav said something about California. I thought he might be headed out your way."

"Not that I know of."

"That's not why you're here," he said, leaning back in the chair.

I glanced at a vase of flowers, the only thing that served as décor in Nick and Jackson's apartment. Emily or Larkin had probably put them there, hoping to pretty the place up. "I wanted to get your thoughts on something."

"Don't tell me—Parker wants you back."

I let out a humorless laugh, trying not to let on how many times I'd actually fantasized about that possibility, even though I knew it wasn't good for me. "Only if I've suddenly inherited millions or taken a job with some fancy international corporation."

"It's someone else then." He leaned back in his chair, crossing his arms and waiting for me to tell him everything.

Everything about nothing. "There's no girl," I said, even as visions of Violet appeared in my mind.

"I'm out of guesses. What is it?"

Why was I here? Maybe it was Violet. Panic shot up from my core, and faster than I could process what I was about to say, the words, "I got fired," spilled from my mouth.

"From your job?" Jackson looked unsurprised. Like it didn't really matter at all.

"Of course from my job. What else could I get fired from?" I immediately regretted my sarcasm. "Sorry. I didn't mean to take it out on you like that."

Jackson shrugged, taking everything in stride. "I've been fired more times than I can remember. What did you do, show up late too much? Take a three-hour lunch? Sleep with the wrong woman?"

"I had a girlfriend," I reminded him. Parker clearly didn't care that much about me, but I'd been committed to her. "And none of that. I was too good at what I did. I bent the rules too far and made the CEO nervous."

He nodded. "So what? You'll get a new job when you go back."

It was my turn to shrug this time. It sounded easy enough. But the thought of actually *doing* it . . . I didn't know if it was Parker or my own ego, but it wasn't something I was looking forward to. "I guess," I said as I stood. "I should let you get back to your cooking."

Jackson stood and peered into the kitchen. "You want to stay? We'll have plenty, and Nick's over at Larkin's."

I shook my head. Last thing I wanted was to be a third wheel at a romantic dinner. "I've got to get back to the B&B."

"How's that going?" Jackson asked.

"Not as fast as I'd like it to, but it's going to happen." I rested my hand on the doorknob, Violet invading every thought in my head again. "Hey, you haven't heard about the county doing some eminent domain thing nearby, have you?"

"Gabe mentioned something about that. He saw it on the town council agenda earlier."

I nodded. "It's got Violet all riled up. It has something to do with one of Chestnut Moon's properties. I might just have to pay a visit to that meeting."

Jackson made a face. "Better you than me. I can't think of a worse way to spend an evening."

I laughed. I couldn't either, but if Violet had to be there, I would too. "Say bye to Emily for me."

Jackson waved and shut the door behind me.

I felt a little lighter, and I took the long way walking back to the B&B, stopping to grab a burger on the way. I was getting used to the stares, locals surprised to see yet another Harker resurface in Bent Creek. I gave each one of them a warm smile and a wave, and the stares quickly turned into a hello or at least a smile in return.

Even saddled with my last name, I was good at winning people to my side. I just needed a little more time with Violet.

She was still on my mind when I got back to the bed and breakfast.

The place was silent as I made my way upstairs. Even Suzanne, who usually sat in the living room area just waiting to strike up a conversation, must have already turned in. With a glance down the hallway toward Violet's room—I'd figured out which one was hers easily enough when we left for breakfast at the same time this morning—I fitted my key into the lock and stepped inside my dark room.

I flipped on the lights quickly to keep from tripping over one of the antique end tables or knocking over a frou-frou lamp. I could hear Parker's voice in my head, complaining about dust collectors and clutter.

I wished I could banish thoughts of her from my mind forever. But the more I thought about her, the more I realized how much we didn't agree on stuff. I would've let her complain, but secretly thought that this place was kind of cute. I didn't want to decorate my apartment like this B&B, but I could appreciate it for what it was. Parker would've just hated it outright.

Dropping my wallet and phone on the night table by the bed, I shrugged off my jacket and shirt. It was early to call it a night, but it wasn't like I had anything else to do. I wasn't in the mood to sit in a bar by myself, or worse, fend away people who'd known me as a teenager and now wanted to catch up. Besides, I had plenty to do here. I wanted to know more about this eminent domain thing that had Violet's boss all worked up. And if I wanted to keep my apartment in LA, I needed to pay rent.

I made myself comfortable in bed with my tablet and got to work.

An urgent knock sounded at the door. I jerked my head up as my tablet clattered to the hardwood floor. Blinking in the light, I realized I must have fallen asleep.

The knocking came again, even louder and more hurried.

"Hold on," I muttered, rubbing the sleep from my eyes as I yanked the door open.

And there stood Violet.

I blinked at her, my hand still on the doorknob as my brain raced to wake up. She was in a tank top and cotton shorts, barefoot, and her hair was adorably messy. Her arms were crossed, like she was hoping I wouldn't actually look.

"Oh, no," she said, closing her eyes and turning away. "I'm sorry. I'll just—I shouldn't have bothered you."

I glanced down at myself, realizing I was only wearing the jeans I'd had on earlier.

Biting back a laugh, I leaned against the doorframe. "Clearly it's an emergency, or you wouldn't come knocking on my door at . . ." I glanced at my watch. "One thirty-five a.m. Unless . . ." I let the words trail off until she looked at me again. "Unless you *hoped* to find me—"

"Of course not." She rolled her eyes and then promptly averted them as if I was standing there stark naked. "I locked myself out."

"Well, *that's* interesting." I braced a hand against the opposite side of the doorframe. "What do you want me to do? Break into your room for you? Offer you half my bed?"

In the dim light of the hallway I could still see her face go pink. For someone who presented herself as a tough businesswoman, Violet certainly had a soft side. One that was easily embarrassed. It made me wonder if I was hitting on something that came a little too close to the truth for her.

"I just need to use your phone. I left mine in my room, and I don't want to knock on Suzanne's door and wake up Annie."

"But you'll knock on my door?"

Her eyes finally found mine again. "You don't have a baby. Can I borrow your phone or not?"

I shrugged and straightened. "Sure. But come in so you don't wake up the entire hallway." Never mind that I doubted there were more than one or two other people in the entire B&B.

Violet didn't argue, though. She slipped in beside me, and I closed the door. I grabbed my phone from the night table. I hadn't plugged it in before I dozed off, so it was barely charged. I started to hand it to her, and then pulled it back.

"Are you letting me use it or not?" she said, hand hanging in the air.

"Sure, if you can answer one question for me."

She narrowed her eyes. "What is it?"

"What's this eminent domain thing your boss is so worried about?" I hadn't found much online before I'd passed out, just a reference to the agenda for the town meeting.

She laced her arms together again, frowning. "Fine. I guess you'd find out when the rest of the town does tomorrow anyway. Summit County wants to buy an old ranch property just outside Bent Creek."

My blood went cold. Old ranch property. Outside of Bent Creek. Owned by Chestnut Moon or Willow Cosmos or whoever it was Violet worked for. "*Our* old ranch property," I said carefully.

Violet said nothing, but I could almost swear that a flash of empathy ran across her face.

I was right.

I took a second, forcing a breath in and out. It could be a coincidence—a chunk of land ripe for development just as my brothers wanted it back. Or it could be something else entirely.

"Why?" I finally managed to ask.

"That's two questions." She held out her hand for the phone.

I held on to it, still parsing through my thoughts and the emotions I didn't except to rise with them. I didn't care about that land. What did it matter to me if we actually got it or not? I was only doing this to soothe my ego and gather back what remained of my pride.

But even as I thought the words, it felt as if someone was cutting my heart in two.

"Look, I'm sorry this is happening. If it means anything, you should know we're going to fight it. Selling property to the government is never good business." Her voice was a little softer, and her outstretched hand dipped a little.

Of course they'd fight it. And they probably had the deep pockets to do it. I had to regroup and think through this with my brothers. Starting with the town meeting tomorrow. We'd need to gather all the information we could if we stood any chance of ever getting that land back in the Harker name.

Because I sure as hell wasn't giving up.

"Here." I found the B&B's number and held out the phone. The second Violet's fingers grabbed on to it, I held fast. "Cute pajamas, by the way."

She yanked on the phone, and I let go, chuckling.

"You'd better enjoy looking," she replied. "Because this is the only time you're ever going to see them."

Chapter Eight

Marybeth

Gabe's hand tightened around mine as we surveyed the room. I'd never seen so many people show up for a town council meeting. Then again, I think I'd been to exactly two before this—once when I was opening Bent Creek Christmas and once when the big topic for discussion was a fountain the previous mayor wanted to install right in the middle of the intersection of Main and First Streets.

"There's Ward." Gabe pointed toward the far side of the room, a few rows back from the front.

We made our way toward him slowly, stopping to say hi to everyone from my first grade teacher to Kyle Clemmons, the real estate agent we'd gone to school with and who was now helping Gabe and his brothers as best he could with information about the ranch property.

Gabe slid into the empty seat next to Ward, and I sat beside him, at the end of the row. They launched immediately into conversation about the eminent domain problem, even though they'd already hashed what little we knew about it to death.

I scanned the front of the room. The same people had served on the town council since I was a kid, with the exception of the only person under forty—Samantha Farrow, who had been a couple of years behind me in school and thick as thieves with Gabe's younger brother Colt. And the only reason she'd made it onto the council was because ninety-year-old Harold Rivera had passed away last year. When you got elected in Bent Creek, you kept getting elected until you died or moved away.

The front rows were filled with the parents of people I'd grown up with. Police officer Robert Scott, in his civilian clothes, kept turning to eye Gabe and Ward. I was pretty sure it was still his life's mission to toss Jackson into the town jail. My mother's good friends, Mrs. Adams and Mrs. Garcia, smiled at me when they caught my gaze. And then my curious eyes widened.

I blinked a couple of times, but he was still there, at the end of the middle row. My brother.

Luke caught my eye, probably feeling my stare. We hadn't spoken at all since I found out that he was behind not only alerting Violet Barnes to Jackson and Emily staying in the old Harker house, but also convincing our brother Drake to set the fire in the decrepit barn on the Harker property. When I'd confronted him, he cut me out of his life altogether.

I hadn't gathered the courage yet to ask him about the chickens. And seeing him now . . . I was angry with him, but sad too. I wished I could scream at him, or at least ice him out with no feelings attached, but I couldn't.

He was my brother, after all. And I'd been the one who had held him up after his wife died in a car accident two years ago.

So instead of glaring at him, I raised my hand in a little wave.

He frowned, his gaze going to Gabe and Ward at my side. And then he turned around without so much as acknowledging me.

I slumped back into my chair and crossed my arms. Luke was probably here to root for the eminent domain action. He hated the Harkers enough to support the destruction of the only thing they wanted, and I doubted he cared whether it was a shopping mall or a road that took its place.

"Ladies and gentlemen, if you can take your seats, we'll get started." Mayor Barry stood at the podium in the front of the room and spoke into a tinny little microphone.

"Didn't we used to dunk her at the county fair?" Ward whispered.

Gabe nodded, and I covered my mouth to hide a smile. Mayor Barry had done everything in this town, from teaching to volunteering at the dunking booth.

She moved the council quickly through the usual things, reading the minutes and the treasurer's report. They launched into discussing old business, which was an unexciting array of broken ordinances and budget approval.

"Now we'll move on to new business and the reason I suspect so many of you showed up for your first town council meeting." Mayor Barry smiled into the audience and was awarded with a few laughs.

The door behind us closed quietly, and Gabe twisted in his seat. He immediately elbowed Ward. I turned to see who'd snuck in for the only interesting part of the meeting.

Violet Barnes stood in the back of the room, scouting out chairs, and finally finding one two rows behind us. She was impeccably dressed, as usual, with perfectly done makeup and not a single hair out of place. I ran a hand over my new Christmas sweatshirt—gotta advertise at these kinds of meetings—feeling weirdly under-dressed.

Across from Gabe, Ward twisted back around and leaned forward, his attention squarely on the mayor.

"This is an eminent domain action regarding the old Harker property outside of town," Mayor Barry said. "Let me remind you that this is a county-level decision, and there is nothing the town council or I can do except relay the town's opinion on the action to county officials. This is more of an opportunity to learn about the county's plans and to gather public opinion. If the consensus is strong enough one way or the other, we may have some influence over what happens next. However, that is not guaranteed. Please hold your questions until the end. First, we'll hear from a resident in favor of the action."

Luke stood, and my mouth went dry.

He made his way up to the podium. I felt Gabe's eyes on me, and when I turned to look at him, he raised his eyebrows in a question. I shook my head. How could I have known about this?

He took hold of my hand before fixing a frown at Luke's presence at the podium.

My brother shot his most winning smile out at the audience, and for a half a moment, it felt like those few golden years after high school. When he'd begun to take over the ranch from Dad, when the war with the Harkers was over, when everyone in our family still lived in Bent Creek, when Liz was still alive and she and Luke were planning their wedding.

My heart ached with the happy memories and the knowledge that things would never be the same again.

"Are you okay?" Gabe whispered.

I swallowed and nodded, grateful for his concern.

"I hope you're all having a good evening," Luke said in a friendly voice. His hands rested on the podium, and his sandy hair was somehow tousled and neat at the same time. He looked for all the world like a man with no worries at all.

I wondered if I was the only one who knew it was an act.

"I should've known it was him," Gabe said in a low voice.

I squeezed his hand, thinking the exact same thing. Luke had done everything in his power to drive Gabe and his brothers out of town. I shouldn't be surprised he'd gone this far.

"As you're all aware, we have a large amount of acreage lying vacant just outside of town. And I'm sure some of you have tried to buy it over the years. I did, with no luck."

A few people laughed, and I felt Gabe tense next to me.

"It's a shame to see that much land going to waste," Luke went on. "Since the owner isn't interested in selling, and they don't seem inclined to keep the place up, I thought we might be able to turn this into an economic opportunity for Bent Creek."

People sat up straighter at the word *economic*. If there was one thing Bent Creek sorely needed, it was something to bring in the money.

Ward and Gabe exchanged glances, and I couldn't begin to imagine what they were thinking. This was their family's land, and even though I no longer lived at my own family's ranch, I'd be devastated if the county wanted to buy it for an *economic opportunity*.

"We've got tourists coming into the ski resorts nearby, right?" Luke said, and several people in the audience nodded. "And even more will come as they continue to expand. Why not capitalize on that? Bent Creek needs something new—something these people from New York or Seattle can't get at the ski resorts in summer. Something that will make them want to stay here, visit our town, do some shopping and dining."

People were nodding even more enthusiastically now, and my stomach twisted itself into a pretzel.

"So I reached out to a few people, and it wasn't long before I found a company interested in creating an amusement park, right outside of town. I told them we had the perfect spot for it, and they'd have all the people they wanted paying to enter from Memorial Day to Labor Day—and maybe even later, if the snow holds off. We approached the county officials, and they agreed to purchase the land to then sell to the amusement park folks. Well . . ." Luke paused for dramatic effect, and I could've sworn people leaned forward in their seats.

"You can guess how that went," he said with a chuckle, and more people laughed this time.

Gabe's hand tightened around mine, and I glanced up to see his set jaw and his eyes fixed on Luke. Gabe was good under pressure, logical and thoughtful, but he was also completely loyal to his family—and all he'd wanted since he'd come back to Bent Creek was to get the ranch back into the Harker name.

Luke had fought him every step of the way, and now it seemed like he was getting the entire town on his side.

"So the county agreed to pursue eminent domain, since they can see how beneficial this will be to our community. And if all goes as it should, we should be breaking ground on Thrill Mountain next spring." Luke stepped back as people began quietly chattering in the audience.

Mayor Barry took Luke's place at the podium and began to field questions from the council members and the audience.

I stayed quiet, even though all I wanted to do was run up and shake my brother until he came to his senses. Gabe sat perfectly still, his shoulders tense, while Ward watched the people asking questions through shrewd eyes. I glanced back at Violet Barnes. She sat up straight, her legs crossed, and not a flicker of emotion showing on her face.

People asked questions about traffic and noise, light pollution, and how the construction would affect nearby livestock. A few people wanted to know if residents would get discounted admission.

No one mentioned the Harkers.

Finally, as it appeared the questions were winding down, Mayor Barry called for a vote from the council on a resolution to support the action. I bit down on my lip as every councilperson except Samantha Farrow, who cited a vague history explanation, and Edward Lipscomb, who insisted the noise and lights would turn Bent Creek into Orlando, voted in favor of the resolution.

"Resolution supporting the eminent domain action against the old Harker ranch passed," the mayor said with efficiency. Clearly ready to call it a night, she opened her mouth—but Ward jumped up before she could speak.

"Mr. Harker?" she said.

Ward smoothed his face into a smile with practiced ease. He paused a moment, and I had the distinct impression he was swallowing the words he really wanted to say. "I commend you all for discussing this topic at a public meeting. I know there are a few of us in the audience with differing opinions." He glanced pointedly at Violet, who hadn't spoken a word and still sat ramrod straight in her chair. "But I know we all want what's best for Bent Creek, and if this is the way it needs to go, it's the way it needs to go."

He offered a warm smile to everyone while Gabe and I sat there, slack-jawed, and others watched him with varying degrees of curiosity.

"Please tell me you don't really mean that," Gabe said in a low voice when Ward sat back down.

"Not a word of it," Ward replied while his gaze wandered back to Violet. "But I have the feeling that the enemy of our enemy is about to become our friend, and I don't want anyone else to see that coming just yet."

Chapter Nine

Violet

I had just paid for my lunch at the Snowshoe Café when Mac called again. I answered the phone as I gathered up my purse and walked outside into an overcast afternoon.

"Did you get my email?" I'd sent him a detailed overview of what had happened at the town meeting when I got back to the B&B last night.

"I did. Thank you for your prompt action on that."

I glowed, standing there outside the café on Main Street while the clouds moved quickly across the sky above me. "You're welcome. I thought that the sooner you had the information, the sooner we could act. I have a few ideas—"

"I met with the board this morning," Mac said as I swallowed the great ideas I'd come up with late last night and early this morning. "They decided upon a somewhat unusual course of action."

"They did?" I stepped aside to allow a couple to go inside the café.

"It's a genius idea, and I think it'll work. The town is in favor of turning that land into an amusement park, right?"

"Yes," I said, even though it wasn't a question.

"The county has already started legal action. We got notice yesterday that they've filed suit to begin condemnation."

That didn't sound good. I crossed the sidewalk to stand between one of the rustic wooden benches and an old-timey streetlight. Across the road, I recognized Marybeth Noble, coffee cup in hand, most likely walking toward her Christmas shop. Her gaze caught mine, and then she quickly looked away. I wondered what she thought of all of this. She'd sat with the Harkers last night, even as the man I'd finally learned was her brother—not her husband—spoke in favor of the action. I'd thought that was interesting, but it explained why she'd been so cold to me in the coffee shop.

"Barnes, did you hear me?"

"No, sorry, Mac. You broke up," I said, my attention back on the call.

"I was saying that we have only two real courses of action: fight it out in court or sway public opinion."

I nodded. It made sense to me. "What do you want me to do?"

"We'll do everything we can in court, of course, but it's the public opinion situation we need you to take care of."

That would be interesting. People in Bent Creek had been nice enough to me, but not overly warm. With the exception of Marybeth and her barista friend, anyway. I was pretty sure most people in town knew what I was here to do, and equally certain that not all of them appreciated an outsider negotiating land deals.

"Okay," I said slowly. "I've gotten to know a few people here. I can—"

"Barnes, have you got a boyfriend?"

I was pretty sure my mouth fell open at the question. Mac was nearly twice my age. Was he seriously about to ask me out? Right in the middle of a work call? "I, well . . . I mean, *no*, but—"

"Good. That makes this easier. We want you to marry Ward Harker."

All the air left my body. I felt for the edge of the bench, and slowly sat down. I must've misheard. There was *no way* my boss was asking me to get married.

"Are you there? Barnes?"

I let out a deep breath. "Yes, I'm here. I'm sorry, I don't understand." *Because you couldn't possibly have said the words I thought I heard.*

"It wouldn't be forever. Just long enough to convince the town that this eminent domain thing is BS. You don't have to fall in love with him or anything." Mac chuckled, like this entire idea wasn't a big deal at all.

"You're serious." It was all I could think of to say.

"Look, if he's as pissed about this as we are, we can use him. His family's got a long history in that town, right? They're trying to make good now, and people seem to be accepting." Mac basically quoted my email back to me.

"Yeah . . ."

"You're a Montana girl," he said, like the state was the size of Rhode Island. "They'll like you too, especially once it looks like you're putting down roots with one of their own."

My heart tripped over itself at the thought of seeing Ward all the time. Living with him, eating meals with him, making conversation with him. What would we talk about?

And *why* was I even considering this?

"No," I said, much too loudly as I stood from the bench. A man I didn't recognize from across the street turned and stared at me. I lowered my voice and continued. "I can't do that. It's impossible."

"Nothing's impossible," Mac said, some of the humor gone from his voice.

"*This* is. I can't marry him. For heaven's sake, I don't even like the guy. He's a snake, and I don't know if half the things he says are true. And I haven't told you everything about his family's history here. I've done some research since he showed up—"

"I know the history," Mac said. Of course he did. He probably spent this morning reading up on it, after the board came up with this supposedly ingenious idea. "It's in the past. Like you said, the town seems to have accepted them back. With the exception of that Noble character, but that's fine. We don't need to convince him. We need the rest of the town on our side. That's the only thing, with the exception of any legal loophole we can dig up, that can possibly stop this."

I wrapped my free hand across my body. I could *not* do this. I had to find a way to convince Mac that it wouldn't work. Or . . . that it wasn't that important at all. "It's one piece of land. We hold acres and acres. Did the board consider just letting this one go? Accepting the county's offer and moving on? I'm sure there's some other property, tons of other properties—"

"We're not letting it go."

"Why not? What's so special about this property that we can't find somewhere else?"

"I don't know all the answers, Barnes. I'm just running this company as I'm told to. The board won't let go of this property, period. You're going to marry Harker, and you're going to do your job."

"But—"

"If you want your job, that is. If you don't, then I'm sure we can work that out."

My body turned to ice, and I hugged my arm tighter around myself. Above me, the clouds swirled like they knew what would happen to my family if I lost this job. "I want the job."

"Good. Let me know when the wedding is." And with that, Mac hung up.

I stared at the phone in my hand. I couldn't do this.

No way could I marry Ward Harker.

How was I even supposed to make it happen? Propose it like a business opportunity? Which I guess it was, but still . . . None of my childhood wedding dreams started with me proposing a business-like marriage to some shark like Ward.

I could find a new job. I had experience now. Surely that counted for something, even without a degree. I could talk my way into somewhere new, just like I'd talked myself into Chestnut Moon.

My phone buzzed with a text.

Don't forget who paid the property taxes for that house in Missoula for the past three years. Good luck with the proposal!

I wanted to scream. To throw my phone into the street and hit something. It was just like Mac knew exactly what I was thinking, bringing up the property taxes as a threat. I knew enough about real estate to know that the company could turn that into a lien on my parents' house, demand repayment, and then force a sale when we couldn't pay.

They had me by my neck, and in that moment, I hated them. Mac, the board, all of them. It didn't matter how much they paid me, they didn't get to control my personal life.

Except they were.

I refused to make a scene on the street, so I started to walk as my thoughts moved as fast as the clouds above. I imagined and discarded idea after idea.

And after hours of walking, I stopped at the B&B and looked up. It was a grand old lady of a house that was older than anyone alive right now. Who knew what sorts of things this house had seen. Marriages, divorces, babies, death—the happiest moments and the very saddest.

She was still here, paint peeling a bit but just as beautiful and strong as ever.

I drew in a deep breath and let it out. If a house, without emotions or memories, could survive this long and endure so much, so could I.

It was just a wedding. An easy one at the courthouse for a short amount of time. It didn't mean anything if my heart wasn't in it. I'd keep my job. Do what I needed to do here. Then we'd divorce quietly and easily, and I'd never have to see him again.

As I climbed the steps to the B&B, that last thought lingered in my mind. And I didn't know why it left me feeling so empty.

Chapter Ten

Ward

Gabe's advice echoed in my mind as I pushed open the door to Mountain Roasters. I'd skipped breakfast at the B&B earlier that morning, and now my brain was screaming for caffeine and my stomach was growling for food. It had been too soon after meeting with my brothers last night—and Gabe's pronouncement—for me to run into Violet. I'd needed time to think, to figure out how to get her to somehow work with me.

I stopped still the second the door shut behind me. My time was up, because there she was, sipping on a steaming mug of coffee at a table in the corner by the window.

Her eyes flicked toward me, and then quickly cut away as she brought the mug to her lips again. That was fine by me. I needed a minute to pull my thoughts together—and to find that caffeine I sorely needed.

"Hey," Larkin said brightly from behind the counter. "Regular coffee?"

I nodded and leaned my hands on the counter. "Has she been there long?"

Larkin didn't need to ask who I meant. "About half an hour. She's on her second cup."

So she'd avoided breakfast too—two days in a row. I couldn't help but think she was trying to avoid me. It wasn't a stretch, considering the last time we'd talked.

The memory of her, sleep-tousled and cute as hell in those pajamas, standing in my room and asking for my help, seared every nerve ending in my body. Beneath all her bravado, I'd left her flustered that night. Enough that she hadn't come down to breakfast the next morning.

Of course, maybe that had more to do with this whole eminent domain thing and her job, but I preferred to think it was me.

"Have you figured out what you're going to say?" Larkin asked as she slid a mug of coffee across the counter to me.

I grimaced and handed her a five-dollar bill. "Not yet."

Larkin took it and opened the drawer. "Maybe you should try just being yourself."

"What do you mean?" I frowned at her. "Of course I act like myself. Who else would I be?"

"I don't mean it like that." She held out my change, but I waved my hand. Dropping it into the tip jar, she continued, "What I mean is don't act like Ward the sleazy businessman. Just be Ward, a regular guy who wants to get to know her."

"Sleazy businessman?" I didn't know whether to laugh or start seriously examining my life.

"It's just an expression. You know what I mean. Don't act all flirty, like you're trying to get something out of her. Just be . . . normal. Like you would with a girl you were dating."

"Normal," I repeated. "So that's how Nick won you back?"

She grinned. "That's none of your business. Go be normal with Violet Barnes. See how she reacts."

I gave her an annoying salute with the tips of my fingers. "Got it. I'll be so normal, she'll be begging me to propose by the time she's done with that cup of coffee."

Larkin rolled her eyes and made a shooing motion with her hand. I took my mug and moved slowly back toward the door—and the table by the front window.

Violet's back was toward me, but I could see her stiffen up as I got closer. She was completely aware that I was coming to sit with her.

Act normal. I wanted to scoff. It wasn't as if I put on an entirely different personality when I talked to her. But it did make me think back to those times when Parker and I were together. It would be late, and we'd be doing something mundane, like watching a movie or cleaning up the kitchen. Those were the only times I'd ever let my guard down around anyone, in those quiet moments of a relationship I trusted.

Except for that moment with Violet in the garden, when I'd told her about Katrina, my stepmom.

Maybe this wouldn't be as hard as I thought. I drew in a breath, put a smile on my face, and took the chair across from Violet.

"Hi," I said.

"Hey." She looked exhausted. Her light brown hair fell in wisps from a ponytail, as if she'd thrown it up hours ago and hadn't looked at it since. There were shadows under her eyes, and she wore a T-shirt and jeans—a far cry from her usual carefully put-together clothing.

It made me feel actually concerned for her well-being. "Are you all right?"

She shrugged. "Are you?"

"What do you mean?" I took a sip of my coffee like I really had no idea.

"Are you telling me that your family isn't scrambling right now? Trying to figure out a way to fight this thing? With how annoying you were trying to buy that land, I'd think you'd be really upset about this."

With Larkin's words and the memory that I'd already shared something important with Violet fresh in my mind, I decided to try the truth. "We are. I am. Can I be honest with you?"

Her eyes narrowed, as if she didn't believe I would be honest with her.

I spread out my hands on the table. "I don't know what to do. For the first time in my life, I have *no* idea what to do to stop this."

She held my gaze for a moment, and then her eyes softened just a little. "Me either."

I could've fallen out of my seat—because I believed her. Maybe this was what Larkin meant. If this went well, I'd owe her more than I could ever repay.

I ran a finger around the top of my mug. "I'm surprised your boss doesn't have some big plan already in motion."

She smirked, but it was half-hearted. "Oh, he does."

"But . . . you're not a part of it? Or you don't like it." When she didn't answer, I frowned. She ducked her head and stared at her coffee. And all I could think of was that guy with the gruff voice I'd heard through her phone the other day screaming at her. My fingers tightened around my mug. "They aren't blaming you for this, are they? Because—"

"No." She looked up quickly and shook her head. "Of course not."

My hands relaxed. "Did they cut you out?"

"No," she said in a voice that made me think that she wished they had.

I was dying of curiosity now. "So it's something you don't like." She said nothing, and I knew I was right. And from the way she looked today, it was something she *really* didn't like. "Is it something illegal?"

She shook her head but locked her eyes on mine. "I know you only care because of how it might affect you and what you want."

Her words were as sharp as the hunting knife Pops had given me when I was twelve, and I winced inwardly. Was that all I cared about?

No, it wasn't. Those memories with Parker were real, at least to me. I wasn't as selfish as Violet was making me out to be.

"That's not all I care about," I said quickly.

"Really. Tell me one thing that means something to you that isn't business and isn't about you." She leaned back in her chair and crossed her arms.

"My brothers." I didn't even have to think about that.

"Why?"

My first instinct was to deflect the question. It was too personal. It required me to dig into a part of me I'd rather leave untouched. But if I was going to get anywhere with Violet, I had to give a little, as uncomfortable as it felt. I almost had to make this feel like a relationship.

I had to be real.

"They're all I have." I took a deep breath to steady myself. I didn't tell many people about our family's past in Bent Creek. It was something I'd rather forget. "How much do you know about my family's history here?"

"A little. Your father's serving time for tax fraud, but should probably have been indicted for more than that. The IRS seized the ranch property. And there's some long-standing disagreement with the Nobles that involved all kinds of nefarious activities."

I shouldn't have been surprised she knew that much. Between gossip and the dirt Chestnut Moon probably dug up on us, it was inevitable. "That's about the gist of it. Dad was arrested toward the end of my sophomore year in high school. My stepmom passed away years earlier, and my mom before that. Besides an aunt in Livingston who took us in, my brothers are the only family I have. I'd do anything for them."

She eyed me for a moment after I stopped speaking, and then nodded. "I have a sister I feel the same way about."

For the first time since meeting her, I heard a waver of emotion in Violet's voice. I wanted to know more—her sister's name, whether she was older or younger, whether they drove each other crazy as kids—but I pinched my mouth shut. I didn't dare push it too far.

She didn't elaborate, and it felt as if she'd closed back up again.

"You were right," she said after a moment of quiet. "About there being some big idea I don't like."

Don't like was probably an understatement, given the way her face paled as she spoke. She looked downright scared. I pushed my mug aside and leaned on the table with my elbows. "You don't have to do it, whatever it is. There are other jobs."

She gave a quick, hollow laugh. "Can I level with you?"

"Of course." I had the feeling I was finally getting somewhere. Like the answer to my question about what to do next would finally be answered.

"I know you and your family don't want that land turned into an amusement park just as much as we don't." She wrapped her hands around her mug, like it would steady her nerves. "We need to work together."

I wanted to jump up, pump my fist, and kiss her right on the lips all at once. *Finally*! It was a step in the right direction. "I agree," I said as smoothly as I could.

"Good." She nodded, and then drew in a visible breath. "My boss—well, actually the entire company board—has an idea. But it can't work without you."

I raised my eyebrows. I couldn't imagine what Chestnut Moon needed me for. I'd swipe that property out from under their noses if I could find a way. "All right. I'm interested." I reached over for my mug and began to take a sip.

"They want us to get married."

The second her words hit my ears, I sucked a mouthful of coffee into my lungs.

Chapter Eleven

Marybeth

I didn't dare go to the ranch to talk to Luke. Especially after he ignored a text and a phone call. *Don't come back*, he'd said a few months ago. If I wanted my chickens, I couldn't go making him even more angry.

I needed to be on neutral ground, somewhere it would be easier to think without a lifetime of memories attached. That place was the sprawling Sav-Time grocery store by the interstate outside of town.

It meant I had to close the shop at five for three days in a row so I could stake out the parking lot. Luke always ran errands in the evening, so I knew it was only a matter of time before he'd need to stock up on food.

My efforts finally paid off on Wednesday when I spotted his old truck in the parking lot. I parked next to him, and after a few minutes, he emerged from the store, pushing a grocery cart. I stepped out of my SUV and waited for him.

When he saw me, he paused for a few seconds. Then shook his head and rolled the cart toward me.

"You following me now?" he asked as he reached for a couple of bags from the cart. "Gotta report back to your boyfriend on my every movement?"

"If you'd respond to my texts, I wouldn't have to show up like this just to talk to you." I grabbed two more bags from his cart and held them out.

"I don't have anything to say to you." He took the bags without so much as a thanks. "I thought I made that clear."

"I'll make it quick, then," I said, biting off a grouchier reply. "Do you care if I take the chickens? We're—I'm building a henhouse." No need to remind him of Gabe. That would only make it less likely for him to agree.

Luke set the bags on the floor of the passenger side, then turned around and shrugged. "Fine by me. I don't have time for them."

I could've slumped against the open door with the relief that surged through me, but instead I turned around and grabbed the last two bags from the cart and handed them to him.

"Is that all the food you got?" I asked when he'd settled them inside and shut the door. For the amount my brother ate when he was working all day, the six bags he'd put inside the truck didn't look like enough to last two days, much less a whole week.

"Trying to cut back," he said shortly, pushing past me to grab the cart.

"You don't need to lose weight." I followed him to the cart corral. He'd lost enough when Liz died, and he was finally looking like himself again.

He laughed. "I'm not trying to lose weight." He turned around and nearly ran into me. "Is there something else you want?" he asked as I took a step backward.

I swallowed around the words stuck in my throat. The ones I hadn't brought up yet but that sat like a wall between us. "I wish you'd reconsider this eminent domain thing."

He hooked his thumbs in his pockets. "It's too late for that. The county took the ball and they're rolling with it."

I pushed my frustration down. "But maybe you can do something now. Instead of riling the town up—"

He raised his eyebrows at me like I was some dumb kid who didn't understand how the world worked. "They *want* it, Marybeth. Everyone else is just as sick as I am at seeing that land go wasted. The town needs an economic boost. And it's *fun*. Something everyone can enjoy."

But it was ripping the heart out of the man I loved.

Luke sighed when I didn't say anything. "Just think. All those people from the resorts will have a new reason to come here. Maybe they'll go ride a few roller coasters, then come into town for dinner and a little shopping."

I pressed my lips together. He knew my shop could use more business. "That doesn't mean we need to get it by stealing land."

"It's not stealing. The company that owns the land will be paid fair and square." He paused. "Unless you're talking about the Harkers, and in that case, no one owes them anything." He said it with such venom that it confirmed exactly what I'd thought from the start.

"You don't care about how this will help the town. That's only a nice fringe benefit. You only pursued this because you *knew* it would drive Gabe crazy. And you're thinking if that property is out of reach, they'll have no reason to stay here."

Luke gazed off into the distance, avoiding my eyes. "They deserve worse than that. I've got to go. Let me know when you're coming to get the chickens."

I stood there next to his empty cart while he jumped into the truck and drove off. I missed my brother. My *real* brother, not this cold shell of a man who seemed driven only by vengeance. Whatever he thought the Harkers did to our family, it was in the past. All of it was so long ago, and we were the ones who got to stay. Who got to grow up in Bent Creek with both of our parents and our family intact. Luke got to inherit an entire ranch.

We won. Meanwhile, Gabe and his brothers had everything taken from them.

Wasn't that enough? I rubbed my eyes, so exhausted from wishing Luke could see that already.

"Hey." A woman's voice made me turn around. Violet Barnes was standing there, purse slung over her shoulder, her hair straight as a pin and her clothes without a single wrinkle. "Are you okay?"

I must have looked ridiculous, standing there alone in a parking lot, lost in thought. "Yeah. Just stressed. Thanks for asking."

She nodded. "Okay. Are you using that?" She pointed at Luke's empty grocery cart.

I shook my head, and she reached for the handle.

"Thanks," she said. And then she smiled at me. "See you later."

I smiled back, because I didn't know what else to do. She headed toward the store with the cart while I tried to figure out why in the world the local representative of Chestnut Moon had been so friendly with me.

Ward must've finally gotten to her.

Chapter Twelve

Violet

The dress was all wrong.

I frowned at myself in the mirror. I should've bought some-thing new. Made a trip to the nearest mall. But to be honest, I hadn't put that much thought into it.

Maybe because that meant I'd have to think about what I was actually doing.

Marrying Ward Harker. A guy I barely knew, much less loved. It could be worse, I supposed. At least Ward was nice to look at. *Really* nice to look at. Smart, unexpectedly deep, resourceful . . .

Also shrewd, and I wasn't ever entirely certain when he was telling the truth and when he was lying through his teeth. Although for a few minutes there yesterday, just before I'd plunged into this business proposal of a marriage, I thought I'd seen something real in him. Some raw emotion he hadn't covered with a sly smile or embellished with the wave of his hand.

It was way more than I'd given him. But then again, I hadn't even trusted the guys I'd dated with more than the flimsiest version of myself. I wasn't about to do more than that with Ward Harker.

I pulled on the collar of the linen shift dress I'd chosen. It wasn't white, but it was summery and flattering. Just very . . . plain. At least my makeup looked appropriate, and my hair was behaving.

A knock came at the door, and I ran nervous hands down the front of my dress before going to let Ward in.

"Hey," I said as I opened the door. "I'm ready. Let me just grab my purse." I found it hanging on the back of my desk chair, and when I turned around, he was staring at me. It only lasted for half a second before he realized what he was doing and cleared his throat.

"You look nice," he said as he shoved a hand into the pocket of his suit pants.

The offhand way he said it made me smile. "So do you." And he did, but I wasn't giving him the satisfaction of seeing me admire how the cut of his suit enhanced every angle of his body, or how badly I wanted to run my hand through his carefully arranged dark hair.

I clenched my right hand into a fist, not entirely sure where that last thought had come from.

"Ladies first," Ward said, stepping aside. He stiffened when I brushed past him, and if I wasn't so worried about smudging my lipstick, I would've bitten down on the smile that overran my face again.

I led the way down the stairs of the B&B, hoping neither Suzanne nor her grandmother would be downstairs to ask questions. But of course, there was Mrs. Dowling, sitting behind the desk, with Pollo the dog asleep in her lap.

"Well, hello, don't you two look nice! Where are you headed?" she asked pleasantly.

"We're—" Ward began, but I cut him off.

"Dinner," I said. "A *very* early dinner."

"How wonderful!" Mrs. Dowling grinned at us. "Are you going to the Lamp Post? Of course you are, if you're dressed in your finest. Be sure to order the filet. It's magnificent!"

"We will," I said, and to my utter astonishment, Ward wrapped an arm around my shoulders.

"After dinner, we're getting married," he said.

My face burned. How dare he just *tell* everyone like that? I wanted to throw off his arm, ignore the warmth that emanated from his body, and tell him exactly what he could do with his wedding.

But I couldn't. Not if I wanted this to work.

So I forced a smile, accepted Mrs. Dowling's congratulations, and let Ward lead me to the door.

The second we were outside, I moved quickly away from him, down the steps. "What was *that* all about?"

"What?" He trotted down the steps after me. "Telling Mrs. Dowling the truth? Not letting her know that the Lamp Post closed when I was a kid? Or . . ." He gave me that devilish smile again, and all I could do was force myself not to huff as I turned around and began walking.

"Where are you going?" he asked as I stomped past the parking spaces out front.

"To the courthouse," I said as I realized the county courthouse was actually in the next town over. Heaven knew I'd been there enough, pulling deeds and filing liens.

Ward stopped next to a slick sports car, some silver thing with a foreign name. He opened the passenger door and waited. Swallowing my annoyance, I strode toward the car and got in.

"Make yourself comfortable," he said as he closed the door after me.

I didn't want to. I wanted to hate this car and the whole smarmy businessman life it came with, but the leather was like butter and every surface inside was gleaming.

We rode in silence until Ward put on some music. I raised my eyebrows as some singer-songwriter country fusion filled the (amazing) speakers.

"You don't like it?" he asked, my expression not lost on him.

"No, it's fine. I guess I had you pegged as more of a slick hip hop kind of guy."

"Really?"

"Or classic rock."

He laughed, and for half a second, I felt more at ease than I had all day.

"I like Zeppelin and Drake as much as the next guy, but this is my go-to," he said as one hand drifted down to rest on the gear shifter. Instantly, I imagined it drifting further to the right and landing on my knee.

My face flared and I looked out the window. "Still a small-town guy," I said to my reflection to distract myself from my earlier thought.

He sucked in an audible breath, and I turned to see him grimacing. "I'd never admit that to anyone, but yeah. I guess it's hard to shake the place where you grew up."

I smiled at that, until I remembered that once all of this was said and done, I'd literally be moving back in with my parents.

"What about you?" he asked. "Still going to live in Missoula when you move?"

I nodded, not wanting to elaborate on that topic. "Don't we need witnesses for this? Although I guess there are people at the courthouse who can do it."

"Oh, Nick and Larkin are meeting us there. They were able to get off work."

"Okay," I said, feeling weirdly outnumbered. Maybe I should've asked Livvy, but of course, that meant I would've actually had to tell her I was doing this.

I wrapped my arms around myself, trying to figure out how I'd share that news later. I'd ask her to keep it to herself. Because the last thing I needed was Mom and Dad knowing I'd married a stranger for the purpose of trying to stop a court action.

"Here we are." Nick parked the car, and I tried to psych myself up as we walked into the courthouse.

You can do this. I repeated the words in my head over and over as we walked inside and Ward made the arrangements. This was for Dad. I'd do anything for him and my family. I reminded myself of that as I signed the marriage license.

Nick and Larkin met us in the courtroom. They laughed and joked with Ward as if everything was perfectly normal while I eyed the judge's chair, the witness stand, and the rows of seating, wondering why I was getting married in the same place where criminals were probably sentenced that morning.

"Violet?" Larkin's voice drew my attention back to her. "Do you need anything? I came prepared." She held up a large purse and shook it. "Lipstick. Hairbrush. Tissues. You name it, I have it. Plus a few toy cars and some broken crayons."

I smiled, appreciating the way she was trying to ease my nerves even though she didn't know me. "I'm fine. Thank you."

She set the purse down on the nearest seat. "So I was talking to Marybeth, and we wanted to apologize to you. I know we haven't been very welcoming."

"It's fine," I said, and I meant it. "I understand."

She nodded. "Okay. Well, I guess we're all in this together now."

The judge arrived then, and before I knew it, the ceremony was underway. The judge was a man older than my father, and his expression was so serious that it made me even more nervous than I already was.

I could hear my heart beat in my ears, drowning out the judge's words. Perspiration beaded at my hairline, threatening to ruin my makeup. But it was hard to care about that when it started to feel as if I couldn't get enough air.

Hands closed around mine, and I realized I was shaking. Ward held firmly to my hands and leaned forward slightly to whisper, "Are you okay?"

His eyes held my gaze, and I focused on the way the clear blue in the middle of his iris gave way to gray around the edges. I breathed in, then out, and nodded. But instead of letting go of my hands, he held on.

Because we were getting married.

"Repeat after me," the judge intoned, and after echoing the vows he spoke, he sentenced us to life—together.

Stop being dramatic. This could all be undone with a few pieces of paper and a court date. Easy.

I realized then that the room was quiet and everyone present—Nick, Larkin, the judge, and the bailiff—were all watching us.

Dutifully, Ward leaned down and planted a perfectly chaste kiss on my lips. It was quick and almost impersonal, but he paused before he straightened. Something smoothed out the shadows on his face, and for a second, I was reminded of the version of him I'd seen briefly at the coffee shop. The same one who'd told me his stepmother had passed away from cancer.

My lips tingled as he dropped my hands, and I had to fight the urge to press my fingers against them. Some wild, neglected part of me wondered what would have happened if that kiss had been anything more. If it had continued beyond a second, or if he'd parted his lips. Would I have stopped it?

Would I have even wanted to?

A burst of adrenaline raced through me as I watched Nick embrace Ward. I'd let my mind wander a little too far down a path of dangerous thinking. If Ward and I were married and pretending it was real, I had to keep my head on straight.

More than anything, I had to remember there was an expiration date to this "relationship." And the most dangerous thing I could do was let myself slide into thinking any of it was real.

Because there was no way I could fall in love with Ward Harker.

Chapter Thirteen

Ward

"Absolutely not." Violet stood at her door inside the B&B with her arms crossed.

We'd been married for two hours, and we were already fighting. That should bode well for the remainder of this partnership.

"Look," I said in a quiet voice. "We're supposed to be married. Married people don't stay in separate rooms. Unless you're wanting to tank this entire idea before it even has a chance?"

She blew air out from between her teeth, sending a wisp of hair flying. I'd never tell her this, mostly because I'd be afraid she'd smack me, but she was awfully cute when she was angry.

"Fine."

"Okay." When she said nothing else, I gestured to her door. "Your place or mine?"

She glanced behind her at the closed door. "Mine, I guess. At least it'll be on the company's dime."

I grinned at her petty victory over Chestnut Moon. "All right. I'll go change and get my stuff. We can let Suzanne know on our way out."

"Our way out?"

"Of course. It's time to see and be seen."

Her face paled, and while I'd never admit it, I felt the same way. People would be staring at us the second they spotted us holding hands. At least word would travel fast without us having to do much of anything.

I changed into jeans and a black button-down, and made quick work of packing up everything I'd brought. Violet ushered me into her room after looking both ways down the hallway.

"We aren't sneaking around," I said, grinning as I dropped my suitcase and work bag onto her floor.

"I know. Just . . . putting it off a little." She'd changed into a pair of curve-hugging light denim jeans and a soft purple top. I thought I'd miss the dress, but I had to admit she looked just as good in jeans. "What are you staring at?"

"My wife." I said it more to annoy her than anything, but it felt nice rolling off my tongue.

Violet rolled her eyes and grabbed her purse. "Where are we going?"

I shrugged. "Let's take a walk and find out."

The late-afternoon sun was warm, and there was only a hint of rain clouds on the horizon. When we reached the sidewalk, I took Violet's hand. She immediately tried to pull away, but I held on. "Married, remember?"

"Right." She sounded so resigned that it bit away at my ego.

"It won't be for long," I said, giving into the bitterness for just a moment.

Her hand wrapped more firmly around mine. I didn't know what to make of that, and when I looked at her, she turned away and pointed down the road. "Main Street?"

"Sure." It didn't take long to walk down the quiet sidewalk to Main Street. Violet turned to the left, toward the town square, and I went along with it. We had no destination in mind, after all.

I didn't know how many times I'd walked down this street as a kid. So many I'd lost track. But none of them compared to this one. I'd never had a woman as beautiful as Violet on my arm, and I'd never been so self-conscious—even after Pops had been arrested.

Violet's chin was tilted up, ready for the onslaught of stares. I took my cue from her and looked straight ahead. The very first person we ran into was Mrs. Foley, Emily's mother, who I'd known since forever. She stopped still in her tracks after leaving the café, and then she smiled at us. I supposed she was the perfect person to encounter first. Since her daughter was dating Jackson, she was already inclined to like me.

I hoped.

"Ward," she said warmly as we approached. "It's good to have you back in town."

"Hello, Mrs. Foley. You haven't changed at all—how do you do that?"

She laughed and waved a hand. "Keep your flirting for your girl-friend," she said with a glance at Violet.

"Violet is my wife." I couldn't believe how easy it was to say. It was almost as if I couldn't wait to tell her. "We were just married."

Mrs. Foley clapped her hands together. "Oh, how wonderful! I'm sorry to have missed the wedding."

"Everyone did," I said as I looked at Violet with what I hoped was loving adoration. "Vi and I wanted something private, and we figured it was now or never, so we just drove on up to the courthouse."

"That's *very* romantic," Mrs. Foley said as Violet stared me down. I'd have to work with her on the loving adoration thing.

"It was," I said, my voice dripping in honey, although I wouldn't have called that imposing courtroom romantic.

"I have a gift for you two." Mrs. Foley tapped me on the chest with the finger. "I know just the thing."

"You don't have to do that," Violet said, finally speaking up.

"Nonsense. I'll see you soon!" She walked away, positively glowing.

"I think she may be the nicest person I've ever met," Violet said as we continued walking.

"She's always been that way. Used to bake cookies and bring them to her job at the bank to hand out to kids who came in with their parents." I could still taste those chocolate chips melting in my mouth.

Violet smiled. "Who's that?" She pointed at a man sweeping out a doorway across the street.

"Old Man Lewis," I said as I raised a hand to acknowledge him. "Runs the hardware store with his son now, I think is what Jackson told me." Melvin Lewis paused, and while he was too far away for me to see clearly, I was pretty sure he was squinting at us. Finally he lifted a hand to wave.

"That was interesting," I said in a low voice. When Violet looked at me with a question written across her face, I added, "He never really liked us. Jackson had a penchant for walking out of that store with things in his pockets."

Violet raised her eyebrows.

"He grew up," I said, a defensive edge creeping into my voice.

"I have the feeling that Jackson could be holding up a bank as we speak, but you'd defend him up and down and back again," she said, a note of amusement in her voice.

I wanted to say no. But instead I laughed. Because she was right. "Good thing for me he's changed. Just the occasional fight these days."

"Plus a little breaking and entering," she countered.

"Hey, that was all on the up and up."

She leveled a look at me, and I shrugged.

"Tell me you wouldn't do the same for your family," I said.

She bit down on her lip then, looking away. I'd touched a nerve with that one. I was dying of curiosity, but lucky for Violet, I spotted Samantha Farrow from the town council headed our way with Flannery Jacobs, who was pushing a stroller.

"Ready?" I said, stopping right where we were on the sidewalk and dropping my hands to Violet's waist.

She gave a little squeak as my fingers curved around the soft fabric of her shirt. "What are you doing?" Her eyes darted up to mine.

I held her gaze. "I don't know what kind of relationships you've had, but in my experience, people who are in love can't keep their hands off each other."

She hesitated, her cheeks going a light shade of pink, and then slowly brought her hands up to rest behind my neck. I steeled myself against the feather-light touch of her fingers against my skin. I stepped forward and she stiffened.

"You're going to have to relax or no one is going to buy this," I whispered.

"I *am* relaxed," she said in the least relaxed voice ever. But her spine curved just a little, and her jaw seemed less tense.

"Better." I snuck a quick glance down the sidewalk. Flannery and Sam were getting closer. "Time for the real show."

"The real wha—?"

I cut off her question with a swift duck of my head, pressing my lips to hers. A strangled sound came from the back of her throat as her eyes went wide.

"*Relax.*" I breathed the word out, hesitating to go any further until her eyes finally closed. I tested the kiss again with a light brush across her lips. She didn't back up and slap me, which would've doomed our pretend relationship. That was a good sign. I tried again, this time with more pressure. Her mouth parted beneath mine, and what felt like a bolt of lightning shot through me from head to toe.

I tried to hold back. I didn't want to give her any reason to wish she hadn't agreed to do this, but the press of her lips against mine, the ragged hitch of her breathing, and a screaming desire to pull her closer drowned out any caution I should have exercised.

My hands tightened around Violet's waist, wondering if the skin beneath was softer than the fabric of her shirt. I gave in to the need to have her closer, pulling her toward me before losing myself completely in the kiss. I was barely aware of her fingers pressing against the back of my neck and lacing into my hair, and I didn't remember *why* we were doing this.

All I knew was that I needed it—I needed *her*. I didn't care about anything beyond that.

"Ward." My name smothered against her lips as I tilted my head for a better angle. Another moment passed. Her hands slid away from my neck, leaving my skin cold even in the warm air. They found my chest and gently pushed.

And before I knew it, she was looking at me, lips parted and swollen and breath coming quickly. Her hands remained on my chest, keeping me at a distance. "I think they're gone," she said, her words barely audible.

They. It took my brain a few seconds to catch up. Flannery and Sam. The reason we were doing this. Right.

I glanced down the sidewalk toward their retreating backs. It was over. There was no more good reason to draw Violet back toward me and pick up where we left off.

I reluctantly dropped my hands from her waist. This was a business arrangement. Nothing more. If it came with a great kiss, I wasn't going to complain.

But I also wasn't going to lose my head over it.

"Mission accomplished." I tried to make my voice sound as distant as possible.

A frown flickered on Violet's face before she nodded. She pressed a stray lock of hair behind her ear. "I need to get back to work."

The words were like a bucket of cold water over my head. And they were exactly what I needed to hear. "All right. I'll go by the diner and get take-out for dinner later. Any requests?"

"Surprise me," she said over her shoulder as she walked away.

Easier said than done, considering she'd already surprised me.

Chapter Fourteen

Violet

I glared at Mac's text on my phone screen. *Good work. Make that town fall in love with you.*

It was like he wanted me to work magic. Missoula wasn't exactly a small town, but I knew how places like Bent Creek worked. You were a stranger if your family hadn't been here for at least three generations. Which basically meant they'd never consider me one of their own.

But that wasn't the case for Ward.

It didn't matter what kind of old history his family had here, I saw the way people reacted to him on the street. They were genuinely happy to see him again. All I could hope was that some of that affection would rub off on me as his wife, and that the town would fight against eminent domain to protect one of their own.

I set the phone down and leaned against the stiff back of the desk chair to stretch. It was late. Ward had brought back dinner hours ago. A burger, a huge chef salad, a hot turkey sandwich, falafel—which I'd never expected to see in a town this small—and six different sides.

"I didn't know what you'd want," he'd said with a shrug as I gaped at the sheer amount of food.

We'd eaten picnic-style on the floor, passing the boxes back and forth to sample everything. And then, as if that wasn't enough food, he pulled out two slices of lemon cake from a bag I hadn't noticed.

"Weddings call for cake, right?" he'd said before passing me a slice and a fork.

I didn't think my stomach would ever recover from that much food.

I hoisted my overfed self from the desk chair and shut the lid of my laptop. The ornate clock on one of the end tables was creeping toward eleven p.m., but Ward hadn't yet returned from visiting his brother Gabe.

My eyes widened as I realized I had an opportunity. We hadn't discussed sleeping arrangements, although the only place to sleep in this room besides the bed was the floor. But the last thing I wanted to endure was a discussion about it.

Especially after that kiss.

If I was asleep before he got back, there would be no discussion. I snagged my pajamas and jogged to the bathroom. I had them on in record time. I splashed water on my face, and patted it dry with a towel. Did my lips actually look bigger after that kiss? Was that even possible?

I pressed a finger to them and told myself I was crazy. But that didn't stop the memory of his hot breath on my mouth, the press of his hands against my waist, and the almost greedy way he'd pulled me closer to him.

I hated to admit it, but it was a good kiss. A *really* good kiss. Even worse, I hadn't lost myself like that since I'd dated Tad Blackman a couple of years ago, but any good memories of him were tainted when he'd dropped me after a few months to go back to his ex-girlfriend.

No, that kiss with Ward was *much* better than anything I'd had with Tad. It felt like my skin caught fire with every move he'd made. I hadn't even worried about anyone watching us, or why we were doing what we were. All I could think of was *him*.

It was a heady feeling, and even reliving it now, I had to grab on to the edges of the countertop.

"Pull it together, Violet," I said to my reflection. I couldn't forget this was an arrangement. That despite the few moments I'd seen something real in Ward, he was really a snake in disguise.

Or was the snake the disguise?

I shook my head at my reflection, more confused than ever. I flew through brushing my teeth and hair, and threw open the door to the bedroom, ready to dive into bed.

Except there he was.

A smile curved up the lips I'd been thinking about nonstop since this afternoon. "You were wrong," he said.

I blinked at him. "What?"

He leaned forward, that woodsmoke and soap scent of him sending my mind right back to thoughts of kissing. "I did get to see those pajamas again."

That's it. I was going straight to the nearest store tomorrow and buying long pants and baggy shirts to sleep in. For now, I acted like I didn't even hear him, whisking past to collect my phone and plug it into the charger.

Ward laughed and disappeared into the bathroom, closing the door behind him.

Letting out a breath, I sank beneath the covers. Maybe my plan would still work, if I could fall asleep quickly. I reached for the lamp and turned off the light.

It didn't work.

There was no way I could fall asleep with my heart hammering like a drum. I'd just have to *pretend* I was asleep. I squeezed my eyes shut, cursed Mac and Chestnut Moon with every breath I took, and tried to look as natural as possible.

After a few minutes, Ward emerged from the bathroom. "Violet?"

His voice was so soft that I almost responded.

Without another word, the bed creaked under his weight, and before I knew it, he was lying next to me. And after a minute or two, I could practically feel the heat radiating from him.

Why didn't this place have king-sized beds? This bed was much too small for me to actually fall asleep with him that close.

"I know you're not asleep." His voice was as soft as kitten's fur, and I swore I could feel his breath on my neck. "Good night, Violet."

And with that, he turned over, and I spent at least two solid hours staring into the darkness and willing my brain to stop wandering places it shouldn't.

"Vi? Wake up. Vioooo-let."

My eyes fluttered open to sunlight streaming into the room—and Ward standing over me, fully dressed, with my phone in his hand.

I sat straight up in bed, blinking away the fog of sleep. "What time is it?"

"Almost nine. Your phone has been ringing non-stop. Who is 'Livvy'?"

I jumped up and grabbed the phone from his hand. "My sister." I hit call back, my heart in my throat. Why would she be calling so early?

"Hey, Violet," she said, answering on the second ring.

"What's wrong? Is Dad okay?" Across from me, Ward watched me with undisguised curiosity. Too late I realized I was in my pajamas. Going out into the hallway for some privacy was a no-go. Instead, I ducked into the bathroom and shut the door.

"He's fine. I'm sorry! I didn't mean to scare you."

I let out a whoosh of air and collapsed against the counter. "What's going on?"

Livvy hesitated. "It's the money."

I smacked my forehead. Between the wedding and dreading the wedding and then . . . other things . . . I'd completely forgotten to transfer Mom the money she needed to pay the second mortgage. "For the mortgage. I am *so* sorry I forgot to send it. I'll do it right away."

"Are you okay, Violet? It's just that you never forget this stuff. Unlike me." She gave a little laugh.

I smiled even as I winced at what I knew I needed to tell her. "I, um . . . well. It's only for my job, but I kind of got married yesterday."

"*What?*"

I had to yank the phone away from my ear at Livvy's reaction.

"I'll tell you more about it later. It's not a real marriage. It's for work." It sounded so lame when I said it out loud.

"Oh, I will be calling you if you don't get back to me soon. Hold on, Gabby," she said to her daughter. "I've got to go. Gabby's got a fistful of markers, and this isn't going to end well."

I hung up with her, after promising to send the money and to call her later. Then I took my time in the bathroom, hoping Ward might go out while I did everything except get dressed.

But as luck would have it, he was right there, relaxing on the bed. And clearly waiting for me.

"Is your dad okay?" he asked, looking up from his tablet.

"He's fine." I went in search of clothes, not wanting Ward to see the truth on my face.

"Is he still sick?"

"No. I have to get moving. I've got so much work to do." I yanked out the first things I laid my eyes on. When I turned around, Ward was standing up and blocking the bathroom door.

"It sounded like something was wrong, the way you were talking to your sister."

I leveled a gaze at him. This was none of his business.

He didn't back down, meeting my eyes and then tilting his head. "Do you need money?"

"What? No! Of course not." I clutched the clothes to my chest. He had to have overheard my conversation with Livvy through the bathroom door. My thoughts raced backward as I tried to figure out how much I had said.

"Does your sister need money? I heard you mention a mortgage."

I was about to tell Ward exactly where he could put his questions, but the look on his face made me wrench my mouth shut. It was the same look I'd seen when he'd spoken about his brothers at the coffee shop.

Unless I was completely losing my ability to read people, it looked like genuine concern.

"I'm sorry," I said, lowering my armload of clothes. "I'm not used to anyone asking me how I am, much less questions about my family."

He shifted his weight, making it clear I could disappear into the bathroom if I wanted to. "Look, I know this is business only. And I barely know you. But I know you're a decent person, Violet, and that phone call confirmed it. If there's anything I can do to help, just let me know."

Tears pricked at the backs of my eyes. No one had ever offered to help. It was me and Livvy and her husband, with Mom and Dad, against the world. Just us.

And here was this stranger—someone I wasn't entirely sure I could trust—offering to help.

I blinked hard and swallowed, shifting the clothes to give myself an excuse to look down. It would be so easy to open up to him. To tell him about Dad, and why I had to keep my job.

But even the moment I thought it, I pushed the idea away. That would make me vulnerable, and I wasn't someone who was weak. *Ever*.

"It's nothing. Everyone's fine."

He eyed me for a moment, and I could almost swear that he looked a little sad. But then it was gone, and he nodded. "All right. But the offer still stands. Tell me if you need anything. Money, whatever."

My throat constricted as I nodded. I didn't trust myself to talk or I was afraid I'd start crying.

"You want breakfast?" he said. "I think we still have a few minutes before they close up the kitchen downstairs."

I shook my head. "I need to work. I'll eat a granola bar."

Ward nodded and then left. I stood there for a few more seconds, trying to figure out what had just happened.

But all I could think was that there was a lot more to this man than I ever could have guessed.

Chapter Fifteen

Marybeth

I wanted my chickens. But I had no desire to go to the ranch alone. I didn't dare bring Gabe. Luke would probably run him off with a shotgun. But if I brought a friend, then maybe Luke would keep his unwanted opinions about my love life to himself.

Larkin had a late shift at the coffee shop, so I enlisted Emily to help me after work and was waiting for her outside the library when Violet came jogging by. She was no longer the enemy, I had to remind myself. She was on our side now—sort of. So I raised my hand to wave.

She stopped, barely winded, in a pair of Lululemon leggings and a perfectly fitted athletic tank. Even her ponytail was still smooth. Meanwhile, every time I went running, I came back looking like I'd spent ten days living outdoors.

"Hi," she said. "Marybeth, right?"

I nodded. "Congratulations on your wedding." Or maybe I shouldn't have said that. It wasn't *real*, after all, and I wasn't sure she really wanted to be congratulated on it.

"Thanks, I guess," she said with a little laugh.

I laughed too, feeling a little more at ease. "Ward doesn't seem too hard to put up with, but I bet he talks a lot."

She pulled a face. "He does. He's awfully nosy too."

"So he's basically the opposite of Gabe." I didn't know if I could've handled that. I much preferred my quieter teddy bear of a man.

"It's not so bad, though," she said, glancing off in the distance.

That was interesting.

"So what are you doing out here?" she asked. "Going to the library?"

"Waiting for a friend. Emily Foley. She's Jackson's girlfriend."

Violet nodded. "I remember Ward mentioning her. Wait . . . Foley. Is she related to—"

"Mrs. Foley? That's her mother. Did you get a bag full of cookies yet?"

Violet simply looked confused, so I took that as a no.

"Don't worry," I said. "It's just a matter of time."

"I'll take your word for it." She tightened her ponytail. "So you're Luke Noble's sister, right?"

"I am," I said carefully. I didn't know where this was headed, but I stiffened up every time I heard Luke's name.

Violet dropped her hands to her hips. "Do you know why he's pushing eminent domain?"

"That's easy," I said with a wry laugh. "He hates the Harkers. It goes way back."

"I know about that. A little, anyway," she amended. "But I was thinking this morning that it's a lot of work for a guy who's tied up in ranching to go so far out of his way to see this through."

"I think you're underestimating the degree of Luke's commitment to driving Gabe and Ward's family out of town," I said as I gave a quick wave to Mrs. Collins across the street.

"This is more than just taking a girl out to dinner and then following up to tell her about people squatting in a property her company owns," Violet said. "I mean, he had to have done some serious research, probably talked to a lawyer or two, found a company interested in development, found a connection in county government, and *then* managed to convince that connection of how important this would be to the area. That's a lot of work."

She was right. It was a ton of work. "And it all happened over the course of just a few months," I said, wondering out loud.

I shouldn't be surprised. It was like Luke had replaced his grief over Liz with an obsessive drive against Gabe's family. I couldn't imagine how much time he'd taken away from the ranch to make all of this happen. With how much he loved that ranch, I never would have thought anything could surpass it. But Luke had surprised me in more ways than one since Gabe and I had gotten together—and never in a good way.

"It occurred to me that it was almost too much work for just a vendetta," Violet went on. "It makes me wonder if there's something else. Some other reason. Something he's getting, or something he needs to keep quiet, or some debt he owes someone. Does any of that sound familiar?"

I shook my head slowly as I wrapped my arms around myself. "No. Luke's whole world is our family ranch."

"Maybe it is a debt, then. Or someone out there has something on him that he'd rather keep quiet." Violet looked lost in thought.

It felt impossible. Luke couldn't have done anything *that* bad. But even as the thought raced through my mind, it was immediately chased by the memory of everything I'd learned recently that I'd never known before. My own family's history in illegal activity that I still didn't understand the full extent of. Luke's presence the night that Nick and

Larkin were shot at back in high school. Dad passing us off as the most upstanding family around, which I fully believed as a kid, when it was just a facade.

I shuddered to think that the Nobles' secrets in this town could run any deeper.

"I hope you're not right," I said honestly.

Her eyes, which were a soft brown, came back to me. "I'm sorry. For your sake, I hope I'm wrong too."

I gave her a thankful smile as Emily called my name from the library steps.

"Hey!" Emily said as she joined us, tossing a purse over her shoulder. "Sorry I took so long. Leo finally went to go live up at his cabin in the mountains, and I've got this new volunteer who's still trying to figure everything out."

"No problem. Emily, did you meet Violet yet?" I dropped my arms to gesture between them.

"I haven't. Hey, I'm Emily Foley."

"Violet Barnes." Violet stuck out her hand and Emily shook it awkwardly.

"So, um, congratulations?" Emily said.

"Thanks. I need to get back to my run. See you both soon." Violet waved and jetted off.

"I don't know what to think of her," Emily said as we walked to Gabe's truck. I'd borrowed it for the day to move the chickens.

"She seems nice enough, once she drops the icy business thing. Honestly, I expected her to be more upset about having to marry Ward." I unlocked the truck and we slid in. "From what he said, it wasn't her idea."

"I sure would be, if I was her. Or Ward," Emily said. "I can't imagine marrying someone I didn't love."

"Me either."

We chatted as we made the drive out to the ranch. As the truck rumbled up the gravel driveway, I hoped Luke would be out somewhere working. It would be so much easier to get this done without him staring me down with all his judgment.

"I didn't realize how close this place is to the old Harker ranch," Emily said as I parked the truck behind one of the ranch hands' mud-splattered pick-ups.

"It's not, really. You have to go a few miles back down the road, take a right, and then turn onto Quarter Mile Road to get there. It's a solid twenty-minute drive. But, as the crow flies, I guess that's sort of right?" I wrinkled my forehead as a distant memory surfaced. "You know, I vaguely remember Dad mentioning that the properties actually shared a short boundary. Somewhere way out that way, I guess." I gestured off to the west as I opened the door.

"I'm surprised no one put up a wall," Emily said.

I laughed. "Me too. I guess it's just too far away to worry about." I glanced around. Everything was quiet, except for the chatter of my hens and the lowing of cattle far off in the distance.

"Is Luke here?" Emily asked, echoing my worries.

"He's probably out working." I grabbed the wire cages I'd bought from the back of the truck and handed a couple to Emily. "Come on, the chickens are this way." I led her down to the coop.

"I can't believe Gabe already built you something," she said as we stepped over patches of mud and muck.

"He was really excited about it. I think he secretly wants chickens too. Hey, girls!" I dropped the cages and made all sorts of ridiculous baby talk to my hens while Emily stood there trying not to laugh.

After we rounded up the chickens—even Santa Cluck, who made Emily chase her around for a good minute—we carried them back to the truck, cage by cage.

I'd just closed the tailgate when Luke appeared, followed by about half the ranch hands he normally had in summer.

"Hey," I said carefully, bracing myself for whatever mood he might be in. "Emily helped me get the chickens."

Emily said hi, and Luke nodded in return. He didn't seem to want to pick a fight, thankfully.

"I think I'm going to miss those little cluckers," he said, gazing at the hens in the truck bed.

I paused, hand on the tailgate, feeling a little guilty. Luke had no one, and here I was, taking the chickens. "Are you sure it's okay that I take them?"

"Of course. I wouldn't have said so if it wasn't." His words were sharp, cutting off my guilt at the root. I'd clearly overstayed my welcome.

"All right, then. We'll be on our way." I started to walk around the truck, as the ranch hands loaded up their own vehicles. Unlike Dad, Luke had always hired guys who lived nearby. No need to provide lodging, and it made for men he could trust more easily.

How hadn't I realized how few trucks were in the driveway when we got here?

"Hey, Luke," I said, curiosity taking hold of me before I climbed into the driver's seat.

He stopped and turned around. "Yeah."

I ignored the edge to his voice. "Where are the other guys? Tony and V and the others?"

He raised an eyebrow, and I couldn't tell if he was annoyed at my question or surprised I'd noticed. "Not that it matters to you anymore, but I didn't hire them back on this year."

"You didn't?" V and Tony had worked for Luke ever since Dad had moved to Florida and given him the ranch to run. "Why not?"

Luke frowned at me. "Why do you want to know? It's my business to run and I'll do as I see fit."

"Right." My fingers dug into the open window frame of the truck door. Never mind that I'd pretty much run the place for upwards of a year. And never mind that even before that, we talked about ranch business all the time.

This wasn't then.

This was now, when my brother wanted nothing to do with me.

"Take the feed too," Luke said over his shoulder as he walked toward the house.

"Thanks," I said bluntly, but Luke didn't hear me.

"Want me to grab it?" Emily said gently from the other side of the truck.

"No, I can get it. Give me just a second." I pushed myself away from the door and headed toward the barn. The last ranch hand to leave, Aaron, waved at me before backing his truck up. I waved back, my mind pushing Luke's coldness off to the side as I wondered again why he wouldn't hire so many of the usual guys back.

How did he have enough people to get the work done around here without them?

It was still on my mind as I loaded the bag of chicken feed into the truck and drove Emily and the chickens back into town.

Something was going on, and I couldn't help but wonder if it had something to do with getting the county to buy the Harker ranch and Violet's speculation that Luke was getting something more out of it.

But *what*?

Chapter Sixteen

Ward

"Look at that!" Violet pointed to a pink flowering plant she'd successfully put into the ground outside the elementary school.

"At what?" I took the opportunity to stand and stretch my back. It had been a long time since I'd done manual labor, and I was feeling it.

"The flower!" She grinned at me like she'd just invented begonias or petunias or whatever these things were called. "I planted it."

I glanced at the flower, its pink petals turned up toward the sky, and tried not to laugh. "You don't garden very often, I take it."

"Never." She stared at the plant in the ground. "Mom used to ask me to help, but I hated getting dirty. Maybe I would have if I'd known it was this much fun. Making something live! Can you imagine?"

I laughed then and shook my head, remembering hours of weeding and watering my stepmom Katrina's garden as a kid. But Violet was right. There was definitely something gratifying about working with the earth and helping living things bloom.

Just as long as I didn't have to do it every day.

"I want to do another one!" she called to Mrs. Garcia, who was overseeing this morning's Beautify Bent Creek experience. I'd signed Violet and myself up to volunteer, thinking that the more people saw us helping around town, the more they'd come to empathize with our side regarding the ranch. I'd never seen such a glare as when I'd told Violet about it. If she was a different kind of girl, I was pretty sure she would have cursed me up a storm.

Another volunteer delivered a tray of the pink flowers, and Violet got back to work, digging and planting and smiling the entire time.

"I *never* thought that would be fun," she said as we walked back toward the middle of town at noon. "Outside, dirt, bugs, *worms*." She made a hilarious face. "I still don't like the worms, but I kind of can't wait to do that again. I wonder if Suzanne needs any help in the garden."

I slid my hand into hers, a routine we were both growing used to now, although I wasn't sure I'd ever be able to do it without thinking of the kiss we'd put on for show that one afternoon. Every time I took her hand, I thought about doing it again. It would be for the town, I'd told myself. But deep down, I knew it really wasn't—and so I didn't let myself go for a repeat.

"I was surprised you owned clothes suitable for gardening." I gestured at her jeans and the old, thin T-shirt that hugged her body just a little too well.

"I thought the same about you," she shot back.

"Yeah, but I grew up on a ranch. I'd never come back here without at least one set of clothes I didn't care about getting dirty."

She was staring at my chest then, and I paused. "What? Wait, are you checking out—"

"Of course *not*." And with one fluid motion, she reached over and plucked a small piece of mulch from my shirt. Just the merest graze of her fingers against my chest sent my mind wandering to places I was trying hard to avoid. I shoved my hand in my pocket to keep from reaching for her wrist and pulling her hand back.

"Thanks," I said, trying not to let any of my real thoughts invade that single word.

"You're welcome." Her eyes lingered on me for a moment before she looked over my shoulder and frowned.

"What is it?" I turned around—and spotted Luke Noble heading our way. "Great."

Violet squeezed my hand. It was strangely comforting as I debated whether to pretend we didn't know he was headed toward us, or just stand here and wait for the inevitable.

"Harker! Violet," he said, stopping in front of us. "Congratulations." He didn't hold out a hand.

"Thanks," I said, tightening my grip around Violet's hand. "We're really happy together."

"I'm sure you are, falling in love after a whole week of knowing each other." He held his gaze on Violet, almost like he was searching for the truth from her.

But Violet just smiled and said, "It was fast, but I knew it was meant to be the second I first laid eyes on him." She looked up at me then, loving adoration plastered all over her face.

She was definitely getting better at that. I dropped her hand and wrapped an arm around her shoulder. It was a move that basically said, *This is mine. Lay off.* I'd never had beef with Luke or any of his brothers before this—I was good at staying out of the family drama in high school—but I wasn't about to let him think he could get anything he wanted from Violet.

He crossed his arms, eyes flicking between us. "It's strange that you didn't want a big wedding, where everyone could attend."

I wasn't going to give him an inch. I'd shut this down so fast, he wasn't going to know what hit him. "We're private people. And unless you're here to apologize to Violet for pushing the county to steal land from her company, we're going to be on our way."

He gave a hollow laugh. "I can see right through this, you know. You're not in love—at least *you're* not in love, Harker. You're using her to get what you want. Maybe you're using each other, I don't know. But if I can see it, everyone else can too."

"No one is *using* anyone," Violet said, her voice harder than normal.

I glanced at her, then dropped my arm and stepped forward, forcing Luke to put space between him and Violet. I wasn't here to pick a fight, but I wasn't about to let him rile her up. We were about the same height, and I eyed him coldly. "She's right. And if you insinuate my marriage is anything less than it is, you'll find yourself wishing you hadn't."

It was something Jackson or Nick might have said. Not me. I was the guy who used logic or twisted words to get out of a bad situation.

But when that situation involved a woman I cared about, I leaned hard into the Harker half of my DNA.

He leveled a gaze at me. "You aren't the fighter in the family, Ward."

"Try me." I stared him down, not wavering. It had been years since I'd been in a fight. I could hold my own back then, and all I could hope was that I hadn't lost it now.

"Are you kidding me? Right here in the middle of town, with your *wife* watching?" He spat out the word like it wasn't worth the effort to speak it.

"From what I heard, an audience didn't stop you from picking a fight with my brother."

His jaw worked, and I knew I'd hit a nerve, bringing that up. He'd goaded Jackson into that fight outside the Pine Street Bar a few months ago. I shouldn't have brought that up, even though seeing him look more irritated did me a lot of good. So I backed off. "Look, I don't want to fight you, and you clearly don't want to fight me. So why don't we just go our separate ways?"

After a moment of silence, he spoke up. "Enjoy your sham of a marriage, while it lasts. It won't get you what you want." He stepped back a couple of paces, and called out to Violet, "You could have done better."

I curled my hands into fists at my sides, watching him saunter away.

"Are you all right?" Violet laid a cautious hand on my arm.

"Yeah." I bit off the end of the word, then forced myself to take a deep breath. "Let's get lunch."

She traced my face with her eyes, as if she didn't believe me. Then she nodded.

We ate mostly in silence at the Snowshoe Café, and I forced myself to make small talk with everyone I knew who stopped by to say hello and congratulations. Unlike Luke, they all seemed to mean it.

His words were an empty threat. People *wanted* to believe in love, even if it was fast and sudden. The idea heartened me, and I polished off two bowls of potato soup before we left to return to the B&B.

We'd just reached the front steps when Violet shouted my name and gripped my arm so tightly, I half expected to see a bruise there later. "Look!" she said.

"What?" I came to a complete halt and twisted around, searching for whatever terrifying thing she'd seen.

"A dog!" She pointed to the side of the B&B, where a fence led back to the garden at the rear of the property. Dropping my arm, she ran in that direction.

"Wait up!" I jogged after her and rounded the corner of the building.

Violet had stopped and crouched down, holding out her hand. "Here puppy, come on! Come see me!"

And then, very slowly, what looked a yellow lab mix trotted toward her, tongue out and tail wagging. Violet immediately began petting it, and the dog rewarded her with several licks to the face.

"Oh, yuck!" Violet said while laughing and rubbing her face. But she didn't stop petting the dog. "Have you seen him before?" she asked me.

"I haven't." I moved toward her and the dog, which didn't have a collar. I leaned down to examine the wriggling creature. "I think it's a girl."

"What are you doing out here, running around?" Violet asked the dog in a high-pitched voice that I'd never heard from her before. "You're so pretty. Yes, you're a pretty dog!"

"Wait here," I said. "I'll go inside and see if Suzanne knows anything about the dog."

In the space of two minutes, I was back outside with Suzanne, who had Annie perched on her hip.

"I think I've seen that one before," Suzanne said. "I don't know who she belongs to though."

"Is there a vet around here we can check with?" I asked. "Maybe scan the dog for a chip?"

"Yeah." Suzanne pointed down the road. "On Fifth Street, about a block north of Main. Dr. Suter. That's where I take Pollo."

The last thing I felt like doing was walking some more, after all that gardening. But if I didn't do something, I was pretty sure Violet was going to bring the dog into the B&B. And I didn't know how well that would go over with Suzanne, especially since she had Pollo.

"I'll take her," I said after I told Violet about the vet. "Why don't you go on upstairs and get cleaned up? Maybe catch up on some work?"

"No way." Violet stood and brushed off her jeans. "I'm going with you to get this baby checked out."

I shrugged. I knew there was no way I was stopping her.

An hour and a half later, I found myself washing a dog in the bathtub of our room at Dowling Bed and Breakfast.

"I can't believe Suzanne said it was okay to bring her inside," Violet said from the doorway. Suzanne had been more than okay—she'd even given us a much too small dog bed and an extra leash. Her only rule was that the pup had to be on a leash if she left our room, in case she didn't get along with Pollo.

"We're not keeping her," I said as I scrubbed the dog's head. The lab slapped her tail against the water, spraying it in all directions. I ducked, but it was too late.

Water dripped off my hair, down my face, and soaked through my shirt.

"I'm sure someone will claim her," Violet said, laughing, as she handed me a towel. "She's too cute to go unclaimed. I'll ask Suzanne to print out some Lost Dog signs for us."

"Do you hear that?" I said, looking the pup in her big brown eyes. "We're going to hang up some signs and find your people. Who are *not* us!"

In response, the dog shot forward and gave me a giant, sloppy kiss on the face.

Chapter Seventeen

Violet

"We have to call her something," I said as Ward gently tugged the dog away from a flowerbed two houses down from the B&B. "Not just Dog."

He made a face. "We're not—"

"I know, we're not keeping her." Except three days had passed and no one had claimed this sweet baby. I'd even called to notify the pound, but still, no one came forward. I didn't understand it, because if I'd lost a dog this wonderful, I'd be a mess until I got her back. "But still, we need to call her something."

"Claire," Ward said after a moment.

"Claire? She's a dog, not a grown woman with a mortgage, two kids, and a job at an accounting firm."

Ward laughed as we continued walking with the dog. "That's what you get from Claire?"

I shrugged. "Names have associations."

"Really." He glanced at me. "What do you associate my name with?"

"You. It doesn't work that way. If I actually know someone with the name, that's what I associate it with."

"All right. How about Happy? You know, because she's happy."

"That's cute, but I don't know . . . Maybe Honey? Or Cookie?"

"She's not food," Ward said, grinning.

I laughed. "Maybe I'm just hungry."

We kept throwing out names until I suggested Barker.

"Absolutely not," he said, wincing a little. "Barker Harker."

I started laughing so hard, I had to lean over right there in the middle of the sidewalk. "First off, I thought you said we weren't keeping her," I managed to say when I caught my breath again. "Second, she could be Barker Barnes. But Barker Harker is too perfect."

"It reminds me of my ex-girlfriend," Ward said, leaning down to pet the dog on the head. "Her name was Parker."

He didn't say anything for a moment, just kept petting the dog, who was more than happy to sit there and enjoy.

"You can tell me what happened," I said. "If you want." I didn't want him to think I was prying.

"It was stupid," Ward said, his eyes on the dog again. "I loved her and she didn't love me."

"That's not stupid," I said, quietly. "It sounds like she didn't deserve you."

He gave me a sad smile. "She'd disagree. Parker had no interest in sticking with a guy who got fired."

"You lost your job?" He'd been busy enough on his tablet that it hadn't crossed my mind that he wasn't employed. But for all I knew, he'd been watching movies.

"Yeah." He stood up and grimaced. "It happened right before I came here. I went a little too far, and they got scared."

"I'm sorry. Both for the job and for Parker, although to be honest, she sounds pretty shallow if she dumped you over losing your job. You're better off without someone like that."

He gave me a half-smile. "You're right. It doesn't make it sting any less, but at least I didn't marry her, right?"

My heart did a cartwheel. He'd married *me*. Someone he didn't love at all. Except . . . My mind flew back to a few days ago, when we'd run into Luke Noble and Ward had called me *a woman he cared about*. I hadn't really thought about it since then. I'd assumed it was part of his act. But . . .

Was it an act?

The way he looked at me now, open and honest and vulnerable, I wasn't sure.

"Barker's a good name," he finally said, glancing down at the dog. "We should call her that."

"Are you sure?" I laid a hand on his arm, and corded muscle contracted beneath my palm. Why did I do that? What was I *doing*? I pulled my hand away quickly.

"Yeah." He reached his arm around me, and tugged me toward him. I felt like Jell-O, molding myself against him, unable to fight the deep yearning I had to fit right there against his chest. So instead, I closed my eyes and breathed in his scent, as he dropped a kiss onto the top of my head. "Thanks for listening, Vi. You know, you can talk to me too. If you ever need to."

His voice rumbled through me, and I clung to it.

When this was all over, I'd hold on to that feeling forever.

Chapter Eighteen

Ward

I felt lighter as I made my way around town the next couple of days. Somehow telling Violet what had happened with Parker and my job had freed something inside me. It was like I'd finally let go of the hopes I'd held on to so hard with Parker, the ones she'd stomped on without even a clue that she'd done it.

"You're like the freaking sunshine," Nick grumbled as he handed me a cup of coffee outside Mountain Roasters. "No one should be that happy this early in the morning."

I shrugged. I'd never really been a morning person, but something about shedding the weight of Parker made mornings more bearable. "I might take up running. You know Violet runs? Almost every day."

Nick raised an eyebrow as he lifted his cup to take a sip. "Only time I'd run is if I was chased by a bear. And then I'd rather just turn around and shoot it."

I laughed as we started walking. "You ran in high school, for football."

"Because Coach made us."

"I don't know. It sounds like good exercise. I guess I could join a gym instead. Violet said she wanted to join a gym."

"You've got a lot to say about Violet."

I glanced at him and he gave me a knowing look. "Of course I do. We're together all the time."

He studied me a moment. "You've got a thing for her."

I wanted to look away, but forced myself not to. Refusing to make eye contact was a telltale sign someone was lying. "I don't."

He stopped in front of the ice cream parlor, his mouth curving up into an obnoxious, older brother smile. "Holy hell, Ward. You do. You *like* her."

I bit back a curse word. Nick was right. He knew me too well to believe any lie that came out of my mouth. "All right. Fine. She's not bad to look at, you know."

"And you're sharing that room," he said, lifting his eyebrows.

"That's none of your business," I replied with a warning tone lacing my voice. "But no. It's not like that."

He held up a hand. "You know her better than I do. Just make sure she's not using *you*."

"I've already thought of that." I wasn't sure where Violet's feelings lay, but I'd studied her enough to figure out what seemed real. It seemed like she was slowly coming around to me.

I just wasn't entirely sure I could trust my instincts.

"I don't suppose she's shared the reason why her company is buying up all this land?" Nick asked.

I shook my head. "I haven't asked. I don't want to scare her off." I had a feeling she'd clam right up if I asked, if she even knew the reason. She stayed tight-lipped about a lot of stuff.

"So . . ." Nick trailed off as we started walking again.

"So?" I replied, curiosity piqued.

"I'm going to propose to Larkin. I think it's time."

"Seriously?" I gave him a brotherly punch on the arm. "Congratulations."

"Congratulate me when she accepts," he said. "I'm thinking the Summer Carnival."

I nodded. "During the fireworks?"

"Right before."

"That's good. How's she going to say no to that?" I shot him a smile to bolster his confidence. I knew he'd been a little pushy with the whole marriage thing with Larkin, and had finally realized a few months ago that he needed to back off and give her some time. I just hoped it had been *enough* time, even though I honestly never could see him with anyone else but her.

"Here's hoping she won't say no." He paused outside Kyle Clemmons' real estate office. "I'm going to stop in and see if Kyle's heard anything about any other deals Chestnut Moon has going on. It can't hurt to keep tabs on that company."

I told Nick I'd see him later and continued down Main Street. My entire goal today was to start selling people on the idea of Violet and me owning the old ranch. They'd seen the two of us together enough, happily "in love." Having Barker out for walks sort of cemented the idea of a family, I hoped. We'd gotten plenty of attention each time we'd walked her around town.

I grinned at nothing as I remembered Violet confessing last night that she hoped no one would surface to claim Barker. I couldn't admit it out loud yet, but that dog was starting to steal my heart too. I just didn't want to think about what might happen to her once we were done here.

I wasn't sure if I could handle leaving her behind.

I pushed that melancholy thought from my mind and waved at Mrs. Garcia and Mrs. Adams. They were older, and had been fixtures in this town forever. They ran half the charitable events, and knew every piece of gossip Bent Creek ever saw.

It was the perfect place to start.

"Good morning, ladies," I said, raising my coffee cup in greeting.

"Good morning, Ward," Mrs. Adams said. She was the taller of the two and had worn the same glasses since before I could remember. "How's that sweet dog of yours?"

"Barker?" I gave her a genuine smile, thinking of how Barker had abandoned the tiny dog bed last night to curl up between Violet and me. "She's great. I just wish we had more room for her to run around, you know? A big dog like that needs lots of exercise."

"Well, you can't stay at the bed and breakfast forever," Mrs. Garcia replied. "Have you started looking for places to rent? A house with a backyard would be perfect. I think my son has a few properties available, if you'd like me to give you his number."

"Honestly, we're thinking we'd rather buy." It wasn't exactly a lie. But I only wanted to buy one property.

"Really?" Mrs. Adams leaned forward, like the gossip would just flow out of me if she got close enough.

She was in luck. Because this was exactly the kind of thing I wanted everyone in town to know.

"I want to get back to my roots, with ranching. And it would mean the world to me and Violet—and our future kids—to have the old property again. She wants to fix up the house, and I'd love to make it a working ranch again. Do it right, you know? Kids grow up so much better when they have space to explore, and a ranch teaches so much about responsibility." I shook my head. "I'm sorry for unloading all of that on you. I just wish things were different."

As I spoke Mrs. Garcia's face grew more and more empathetic, and by the end, Mrs. Adams was shaking her head.

"It's a shame," Mrs. Adams said. "What happened to your family's property."

"Your dad was no good, but you boys seemed to have turned out decent, considering everything," Mrs. Garcia added. "Although I'm not sure about Jackson. He keeps finding himself in scrapes, doesn't he?"

I strangled a laugh in my throat. Mrs. Garcia had always been one to speak her mind, no matter how rude it might come across. But she was right in this situation. Pops had ruined everything, but somehow, we'd all survived. Some deep part of me missed him—the way he'd taught me how to catch a fish and rope cattle and tie my shoes. But all of that was overshadowed by everything that came after.

He'd destroyed our family with his greed, and now we were desperately trying to pick up the pieces.

"Thank you," I said to Mrs. Garcia. "Jackson's staying out of trouble. You know, I wish we could do something about the county buying the property. It's great that the town might benefit from the amusement park, but I'm sure there's someone else willing to sell their property for it. It just seems so wrong that they're taking my family's legacy to make it happen."

Mrs. Adams chewed her lip, and Mrs. Garcia shook her head. I was starting to win them over.

"It'll bring in a lot of money if it happens, but if I'm honest," Mrs. Garcia said, "I'm a little afraid of what a place like that might do to Bent Creek. To the character of it, and what sorts of people it might bring in."

Tourists. Which was what this town survived on. But I wasn't about to say that, considering I wanted her on my side. So I shook my head. "You're right. You never know. Things like that always attract fast-food places and chain hotels too. I wonder what it'll do to places like the B&B and the Snowshoe Café."

Mrs. Garcia nodded sagely. "Definitely something to think about."

"I ought to get home," I said. "Violet's going to wonder where I am."

Mrs. Adams smiled. "We loved having you both volunteer for Beautify Bent Creek. Did you sign up for the Summer Carnival yet? You know we can't make it work without everyone pitching in."

"Not yet, but thank you for the reminder. You can count on the both of us."

The ladies went on their way, and I took a sip of my cooling coffee.

Two down, lots more to go.

Chapter Nineteen

Marybeth

I gave Gabe a quick peck on the lips after we stepped out of the diner. "I'll see you at home later."

His arms wrapped around me and pulled me close to him. "I'd rather come home now."

I touched his nose with the tip of my finger. "If you stand up your brothers for me, I'll never hear the end of it. Go. Have fun!"

"You're my favorite, you know that?" He ducked his head until his forehead touched mine.

"Mmhmm," was all I could say before he caught my mouth in a real kiss. As much as I would have loved to stand there forever, I made myself gently push against his chest. "You're going to be late."

"All right, I'll go." He reluctantly let me go and headed toward Nick and Jackson's apartment, while I turned the other way to go home.

I'd made it a whole block and a half when I spotted a vaguely familiar figure at the end of the block, right in front of the Pine Street Bar.

"Drake?" I said under my breath as I squinted through the dying light of dusk. My brother Drake had just left town to return to Florida a few months ago. We texted often enough that I thought he would've mentioned he was coming back before just showing up again.

"Drake!" I yelled as I drew closer.

He looked up, and I almost stopped in my tracks. It wasn't Drake—it was his twin, Wilder.

What in the world was he doing here?

I hurried toward him as he reached for the side of the building. "Wilder!" I opened my arms to give him a hug.

He pressed away from the building and stumbled forward, landing in my arms in a messy tumble. I wrinkled my nose and pushed him away. He reeked of whiskey, and his normally perfectly tousled brown hair went in all directions.

"You're drunk. Why are you drunk? Why are you *here*? Is this some sort of weird game you've cooked up with Drake, where you guys just show up unannounced to catch me off guard?"

"Marybeth!" His voice was a little slurred, and he had a hard time focusing on my face. "Just who I wanted to see."

"I'm glad to see you too." I grabbed hold of his arm as he stumbled sideways.

"Sorry," he mumbled.

"What are you doing here? Aren't you supposed to be planning a wedding with your fiancée?"

"Ha!" His fake laugh rang off the side of the building. "No wedding. Broke it off."

"Oh." I didn't know what else to say. That explained the drinking, but he could've done that in Florida, where his job and his twin and our parents were. "I'm so sorry. You can tell me what happened later.

For now, let's . . ." I looked around, trying to figure out the best solution. "Let's go to my house. Get you some water."

"I'm not staying with you," he said, reeling backward and almost losing his balance.

I gritted my teeth. Luke was working awfully hard to make sure no one else in the family was okay with me and Gabe being together. At least Drake and I had come to an understanding—he hated it, and I knew it, but we didn't discuss it.

"Okay, then," I said, swallowing my irritation. "Where are you staying?"

"At the ranch."

Of course. The one place I *didn't* want to go. But I couldn't leave him out here. Not like this. Luke would just have to understand. "I'll take you there."

He swayed a little, and then nodded. Ever so slowly, with me holding on to him to keep from tripping or going sideways into a building, I walked him back to my house. We cut across Main Street and took the side streets. The fewer people who saw him like this, the better. The second my SUV in the driveway came into sight, I said a silent thank you for having not run into anyone I knew.

Holding on to Wilder, I unlocked the doors. "In you go," I said as I held his door open. It took a lot of fumbling, but he managed to climb inside.

I settled into the driver's seat, wondering if I could just drop him off without having to get out of the car myself. I could text Luke and let him know Wilder was out front, and then speed off without needing to have some awkward/angry conversation with my oldest brother.

The road to the ranch narrowed as we left town. Wilder reached over and slowly punched buttons on the dash until some music came through the speakers.

"I always liked this song," he said as some '90s love ballad played. "Makayla liked this one too."

I glanced over at him as he stared off into the distance, singing off-key and looking utterly pathetic. "Do you want to tell me about it?" I asked, wondering if maybe I should've waited until he was sober for that question.

"Not much to tell. She was messing around with . . . with . . ." He trailed off, and my heart ached for him. "Doesn't matter. All that cheating. I dumped her. Now she can spend all her time with that asshole." He leaned his head against the back of the seat.

"I'm so sorry, Wilder," I said. I couldn't imagine how devastating that was, to be planning a wedding only to find out your fiancée was cheating on you.

"Nothing to be sorry for," he muttered, his eyes on the dark shadows of the pines and firs lining the narrow road.

He went quiet again, and I let him be. I just wished I could have done something more to cheer him up, but I supposed nothing was going to do that until more time had passed.

"We're here," I said as I turned into the ranch's driveway. The security light flickered on as I pulled up to the garage. I unlocked the doors and hoped he would get out on his own.

When he just leaned his head against the window, I sighed and stepped out. The temperature had dropped as night fell, and I shivered in my short sleeves. Opening his door slowly, I caught his shoulder as he began to fall.

"You're going to have to do this on your own. I can't carry you," I said, leaning my weight against him.

"I can walk." He clumsily got out of the truck, and I grabbed his arm to keep him upright once his feet hit the ground.

"Thanks, Marybeth." He shot me a wobbly smile, and I shook my head.

"Come on." I led him to the house. I hesitated, and then knocked. I tried not to think about how weird it felt to knock on the door here, but I wasn't about to barge in considering how unwelcome Luke had told me I was.

He opened the door in a worn flannel, old jeans, and a serious five-o'clock shadow. His eyes immediately flicked from me to Wilder. Without a word, Luke pushed the door open and stepped aside.

I helped Wilder in far enough for him to grab hold of the kitchen counter.

"Thanks, Marybeth," he said again, a happy smile on his face as if nothing was wrong. I guessed Makayla was a distant memory at the moment, and maybe that was for the best.

"I found him outside the Pine Street Bar. I couldn't leave him there like this, and he didn't want to come back to my place." I hated that I felt the need to explain my presence here. And I hated it even more that I'd braced myself for whatever anger Luke was going to feel the need to throw at me.

"I'm going to bed." Wilder stumbled through the kitchen to the living room.

"If you fall, I'm leaving you in the middle of the floor," Luke called after him.

We both watched as he made it just as far as the couch, where he promptly collapsed.

"Idiot," Luke whispered under his breath.

"He's in pain," I said sharply. "If anyone should understand that, it's you."

"I managed not to drink myself into a stupor."

Instead you disappeared into yourself and left me to take care of everything. I bit back the retort. It wasn't fair—or kind—and I knew it. Who knew how I'd react if something that awful happened to me. Luke might not care now that I was there for him, but I'd never hold that time in his life against him.

"I didn't know he was in town," I said, changing the subject.

Luke shrugged, like it didn't matter whether I knew or not. "Wasn't sure you'd care."

I watched him for a moment, and he crossed his arms defensively. "I do care," I finally said. "More than you know."

When he didn't say anything in return, I started for the door. But then I paused and looked back, realizing something was wrong.

The old grandfather clock was missing. The one Mom claimed some great-great-aunt lugged here in a covered wagon from back East in the 1800s. "Where's the clock?" I asked.

"Sold it," Luke said without a glance behind him.

"What? Why?"

"Because someone wanted to buy it," he said slowly, as if I were especially stupid.

"Luke! That was a family heirloom!" I didn't know if I was mad about the actual clock or the fact that he'd done something like that without consulting the rest of us first.

Or maybe he had—and I was no longer one of "us." Tears stung the corners of my eyes at that thought, but I bit down hard on the inside of my cheek to keep from crying.

"I never really liked it," he said. "Any other questions before you go?" He took a step forward, herding me toward the door.

"No," I said bitterly. "Make sure Wilder drinks some water and takes Tylenol."

Luke took another step forward, and I slipped out the door without so much as a goodbye. I could hear the flip of the deadbolt the second the door shut behind me.

I gave up holding back the tears as I walked to my car. Inside, I swiped at my eyes. It wasn't the first time Luke had been condescending and mean, and it wouldn't be the last, not so long as I chose Gabe.

I turned around and drove back toward home, trying to focus on how weird it was that he'd sold that clock. Except . . . maybe it wasn't so weird. Violet had said she suspected that Luke was getting something out of this eminent domain deal—something more than the satisfaction of seeing the Harkers' land out of their hands forever.

He'd sold a priceless clock. He'd brought back a skeleton crew of ranch hands during the busiest season. He barely bought enough groceries to survive. Stuff he only would've done if he was broke.

Was that it? Was he out of money?

Chapter Twenty

Ward

S ticky red goo dripped down the side of the snow-cone Violet scooped.

"Perfect!" Mrs. Garcia said. "You'll have a line before you know it." She leaned forward to whisper over the booth's counter. "Don't let Mickey do the scooping. He makes a mess. Make him do the tickets."

"Good luck," I said to Violet, grateful that Mrs. Garcia had a different Summer Carnival job for me.

Violet shook the red mess off her hand and waved. "See you in a few hours!"

I blew her a kiss for effect. It worked, because Mrs. Garcia smiled all benevolently at us. "You lovebirds can meet up after your shifts. Now, Ward, I have you just across the way here at the candy booth. It's a popular one. The kids love it."

Thankfully, the candy booth was just handing cups of ping-pong balls to kids and letting them try to knock down pins to win candy. Plus I had a teenager assigned to pick up all the ping-pong balls. Easy.

Or at least that was what I thought until six o'clock rolled around. I'd forgotten how every man, woman, and child within a hundred miles showed up to the Bent Creek Summer Carnival. And I'd forgotten that kids would spend every ticket their parents bought them to load up on candy.

I broke a sweat handing out cup after cup of ping-pong balls and opening and handing out bags and bags of donated candy. One kid walked off using his shirt as a giant bowl to carry his victory loot.

"Gabe and I did that one year," Nick said, watching the boy walk away. He leaned up against the corner of the booth while an earnest girl in pigtails flung three cups' worth of ping-pong balls at the pins. "We conned a few kids out of their tickets and went to town at the candy booth. I'm pretty sure we shut it down."

"I'm *never* doing this again," I said in a barely quiet whisper as some kid screamed for the Laffy Taffy options. I shoved a random one his way before taking a second to glance across at Violet. Every time I caught a glimpse of her, she was grinning her head off or laughing. Like the snow-cone booth was the best thing she'd ever done.

"Miss your wife?" Nick asked with a sly smile.

I didn't answer. I had to deliver cups of ping-pong balls to kids, after all.

"I *hate* this," I said to Nick through my teeth. "Why aren't you volunteering? How'd you get out of it?"

"Oh, I didn't. I did set-up this morning. Pro tip, brother—always volunteer for set-up."

I shook my head, wishing he'd mentioned that earlier before I'd gotten shoved into ping-pong and candy duty. Ignoring the waiting kids, I took a second to stand still. "You still planning to ask Larkin?"

"Yeah." Nick looked oddly queasy. "Right before the fireworks, over by the wishing well. I figure that's a pretty spot."

I reached over and clapped him on the shoulder. "She's going to say yes."

He nodded and rubbed his jaw. "I hope so."

"Want us to show up for moral support?"

Nick shoved his hands into his pockets. "Yeah," he said after a second. "That would be nice. Don't tell anyone else though. Last thing I need is all of you staring at us."

"Mister! I need the tiny Snickers!" a boy shouted and pointed to the pin he'd knocked down.

I rolled my eyes. "Duty calls. I'll see you at the wishing well."

By the time there were ten minutes left in my shift I'd handed out about approximately a million ping-pong balls and just as many pieces of candy, and the kid helping me looked ready to drop.

"Think anyone will notice if we cut out early?" I asked the kid as the line for our booth continued to grow.

His eyes grew wide. "Yes. Mrs. Garcia."

I nodded, carefully considering his words—and decided he was right. I didn't want to get on that woman's bad side.

So I got back to work, holding out three cups to a girl who handed me three tickets. "Hey," I said. "You've already been here at least six times."

"Ten," she said proudly.

I decided I was glad none of these kids were mine. My eyes darted over to Violet's booth again—but she wasn't there. Now *that* wasn't fair. She'd gotten off early. I searched the crowd, looking to see if she was waiting for me nearby.

Not that she *had* to wait for me.

But I kind of hoped she would.

I finally spotted her just past the next booth. She was talking to someone. The crowd shifted and I saw a man in jeans and a cowboy hat. I watched for a moment, even as kids yelled for cups of ping-pong balls.

But the guy stayed put. It was hard to see Violet's expression from here, but she had her hands on her hips. He pulled off his hat and tapped it against his leg. I didn't recognize him from the back, but I'd figured out one thing.

He was hitting on her.

"I'll be right back," I said to the kid in the booth, barely even hearing him call after me.

Violet could hold her own with unwanted attention, I was entirely sure of that. But I wasn't about to leave her alone in case it went sideways.

I strolled through the people, eyes focused on the back of the guy's head. It wasn't until she stepped sideways, and he turned to continue facing her that I realized who he was.

One of the Noble twins.

My back stiffened, and I paused. I didn't know which one it was, and I had no idea why he was here. My brothers had mentioned that one of them had been back in town recently, conveniently timed with the barn on the old property going up in flames.

Maybe he'd never left.

I didn't take my eyes from him as I stepped forward. He swayed slightly, like he'd been drinking.

He reached out, faster than a striking snake, and laid a hand on Violet's arm. My fists clenched. Violet lifted her arm, but he held fast. Blood rushed to my ears.

Enough was enough.

Chapter Twenty-one

Violet

Wilder Noble was drunk. He'd managed to introduce himself, ask me if I was from around here, and tell me about his cheating ex-fiancée all within less than three minutes.

If he was hitting on me, this was a really terrible way to go about it.

"Are you related to Marybeth?" I asked, both out of curiosity and out of a desire to stop his rambling about his ex.

He nodded slowly, his eyes drifting away before coming back to meet mine. "My sister. You friends with her? She's . . . she's . . ." He shook his head, like Marybeth was some kind of lost cause.

"I know Marybeth." I paused and stepped to the side, hoping to randomly spot her in the crowd. "Do you want me to call her?" I didn't have her number, but it would be easy enough to get.

"No," he said kind of sheepishly. "I'm okay." He swayed again and reached out to grab my arm to steady himself.

"I don't think you're okay." I let him linger for a moment before I lifted my arm to try to shake him off. But he hung on like I was a life preserver in the ocean.

"Yes. No." He shook his head, and I could've sworn I saw his eyes go watery.

"Hey," I said gently, giving up on getting him off my arm. "It's going to be—"

I was cut off as someone yanked Wilder's hand off my arm.

"Ward?" I said, surprised because the last I'd seen of him, he was neck-deep in kids at the candy booth.

"Are you all right?" he asked, angry eyes tracing me from head to toe. "Did he hurt you?"

"No, I'm—Ward!"

He'd already turned around and shoved Wilder backward. Wilder couldn't have remained standing, the state he was in. He fell backward, and only the sheer amount of people behind him kept him from hitting the ground.

I pressed my hands to my mouth, eyes wide as I looked back to Ward. I'd only seen him ruffled once, when we'd run into Luke on the street. But even then, he'd remained cool, always the self-assured businessman. But now . . . now he looked like someone else.

Fury etched lines on his face as he glared at Wilder, who had managed to right himself. "That's my *wife* you've got your hands all over."

I stood frozen as Wilder lifted his hands. "I wasn't . . . wasn't . . ." He stumbled over his words.

"Learn how to be respectful. When a woman looks uncomfortable, you *back* off." Ward shoved Wilder again.

I jumped as Wilder fell backward. I didn't know what to do. Short of grabbing hold of Ward and trying to drag him backward, I felt helpless.

"Dammit, Ward!" Nick appeared seemingly out of nowhere. He grabbed his brother by the elbow and dragged him back and away as a bystander helped Wilder stand up.

Nick glanced at me as Ward glared at Wilder. "He's drunk," I said to Nick. "He didn't do anything, but it must've looked like he did."

Nick nodded and pulled Ward back into the crowd. With a glance back at Wilder, who seemed more confused than anything, I followed them.

"You can let me go." Ward yanked against Nick's grip. "I'm fine."

"You didn't look fine. You could've blown everything, you know that?" Nick let him go and Ward shook out his arms before turning to me.

"Are you all right?" He lifted a hand to cup my cheek. I wanted to lean into it and close my eyes. Even more than that, I wanted to take him into my arms and tell him that everything was okay. That even though his instinct was completely misplaced, it meant everything to me that he'd defended me like that. No one had ever done that for me.

But instead, I nodded as I wrapped my arms around myself.

"Did you hear me?" Nick said.

"I heard you." Ward was watching Wilder now, stumbling off into the crowd. Everyone had gone on their way. The spectacle was over. "It's fine."

"Only because I stepped in." Nick threw his hands up. "I never thought I'd be the one pulling *you* away from a fight."

Ward's gaze shot back to his brother. "You didn't have to. I'm not you. I can keep things under control."

"Sure didn't look that way."

"Maybe it didn't, but he needed to know I wasn't going to stand for anyone messing with Violet. I don't care what his last name is."

Nick ran a hand through his hair. "Look. I get it. I hate them too—"

"I *said* it had nothing to do with who he was." Ward laid a stony glare on his brother. "I don't give a damn about any of this family feud,

Hatfields and McCoys crap. But you should be happy about what just happened."

"Why is that? Educate me, Ward. Because all I saw was someone trying to show the entire town that we're nothing worthwhile. That we don't deserve their support when we need it the most."

"Because it makes them look bad! Not us. I was in the right, he was wrong, and his actions rub off on Luke. And that'll make people turn against them."

I looked between them. They both made sense. but I hoped that Ward was right. Because we couldn't afford for Nick's theory to be true.

Nick shook his head. "I don't know. Maybe. Look, I've got things to do, so if I can trust you not to throw a punch at the next Noble you see walking around here . . ." He spoke with a slight smile, and after a moment, Ward actually laughed a little.

"I think I'm good." Ward gestured off to the middle of the field that had been turned into the carnival grounds. "Go. I'll see you soon."

Nick clapped him on the back and left.

I turned to Ward. "I was fine, you know. He didn't do anything wrong."

"He had his hand on you and wouldn't let go. That counts as *wrong* in my book, Vi."

The nickname sent a wave of warmth through me. The affection I was feeling for this man was starting to become a problem. I closed my arms tighter around myself, wishing I could block it off. "He was drunk. He lost his balance and grabbed on to me. That's all."

Ward leveled a gaze at me. "You tried to shake him off and he wouldn't let go."

"It looked that way, but . . . You're right. He didn't let go, but he didn't mean anything bad by it. I know the difference."

"So next time, what? I should just stand there and let you get manhandled? I can't *do* that. You'll have to find yourself another fake husband who doesn't care." He let out an audible breath, looking so frustrated that I could almost feel it as if it was my own.

I dropped my arms and reached for his hand. He let me take it, and then, after a few seconds, squeezed my fingers. "Come on," he said. "I want to get a good spot."

"For the fireworks?" I followed him as he nodded and led me through the people to a less crowded area by what looked like a wishing well.

We stood there for a moment, watching people mill around as the sun began to fade.

I looked up at him, at the storm-colored eyes that drew me in every time I caught his gaze, at the sharp angles of his jaw, at the way his hair laid against his forehead, at the ever-present smile lines on either side of his mouth.

And I felt strangely grateful. I couldn't kid myself that this was a real relationship, much less a marriage. But if I had to be stuck with someone, I couldn't have chosen better.

I didn't know that I'd ever *want* to choose better.

That realization snaked its way through me, challenging me to do something. To make this more than what it was. We'd already fallen across the line from business to . . . something else, more than once.

What did that mean? What did it mean that I hoped it happened again?

"Ward?" I said tentatively.

He looked down at me, still holding my hand.

"Thank you."

"I thought you were angry with me."

I bit down on my lip and shook my head. "I was scared, actually. I've never seen you look like that."

"I'm sorry, I just . . ." He rubbed a hand across his face. "Maybe there's more Harker in me than I like to think there is. I thought I saw something happening, and I wasn't about to let you be treated that way."

"No one's ever stood up for me like that," I confessed. "I always had to stand up for myself."

He gave me a little smile. "And I know that you can. But sometimes, you don't have to. Especially with me."

His hand found my face again, and this time, I gave in. I closed my eyes and leaned into his palm, relishing the feel of his skin against mine. I hadn't even gotten enough of that before I felt the press of his lips against my mouth.

This was what I wanted. It complemented the emotional whirlwind inside of me, gathering up all my feelings and turning them into something new and wonderful and perfect.

His hand cupped my jaw and tilted my face up closer to his, and the kiss quickly turned from gentle to something more urgent. I wrapped my hand around his arm and clung to him. I was drowning like a coin tossed in that well, and I didn't care.

Nothing mattered except him, me, and this moment.

"Violet," he whispered my name against my lips. I rose on my toes to bring him to me again, but he held back. "Vi," he said with a groan. "We can't keep doing this."

"Doing what?" I said, half-dizzy from the intensity of that kiss. "Showing everyone that we're married?"

His hand traced my face, and he gazed down at me with a pained look. "It's more than that. Right?"

I could pretend it wasn't. I could act like he was the only one feeling as if we'd left business behind a long time ago. But I also couldn't do that to him—or to myself. "Right," I said, anxiety tracing the edges of my voice.

"When it ends, I . . ." He shook his head as if he couldn't finish.

But I knew what he was going to say. If we kept going, it was going to hurt us at the end. And there would be an end, one way or the other. His life was in California. Mine was in Missoula and wherever else Chestnut Moon chose to dispatch me to buy up land that had been in families for generations.

Our lives weren't compatible.

"I know," I said reluctantly.

He stepped back, but he never dropped my hand. He was still holding it as a hundred feelings rushed through me. Nick appeared nearby with Larkin, right next to the wishing well. They looked at each other like there was no one else around. And just before the fireworks were about to begin, with the stars peeking out overhead and the mountains black smudges against the night sky, Nick dropped to one knee in front of Larkin.

I bit back a gasp and looked up at Ward. "Did you know about this?"

He shrugged, but the corner of his mouth lifted in a smile. "Maybe."

"You know this, but I'm going to say it again anyway. You're the *only* one for me, Larkin Reyes," Nick said as he held her hand. She blinked rapidly, and I knew she was holding back tears. "All those years we were apart, I still knew that. And when we got back together, I not only fell in love with you, but with your son too. I've waited, and I've worked, and I hope I've proven I can be everything you need. I'd do anything for you. Hell, I even backed off when you asked," he said with a chuckle, and Larkin covered her smile with her hand.

"But I'm not backing off now," he continued. "Because I want you forever. I want Diego forever. Will you marry me?"

He opened up a ring box as Larkin pressed a second hand to her mouth. For a moment, she didn't reply. Everyone around us had gone into a hush, and we waited. Ward squeezed my hand.

"Yes," she finally said, and the crowd let out a collective sigh before cheering.

Nick slid the ring onto her finger before standing and gathering her into a blistering kiss as the first fireworks exploded above.

Tears stung my eyes as I clung to Ward's hand. It was a perfect moment, and the love between them was blindingly evident.

I wanted it for myself, so badly that it almost hurt.

And God help me, I was afraid I wanted it with the man standing right next to me. The one I'd just agreed to keep my distance from.

Chapter Twenty-two

Ward

I'd avoided coming to the old place until now.

Putting the car in park, I sat for a moment with my hands on the steering wheel, just staring. According to my brothers, they'd put a new roof on the house while Jackson was staying here. And Jackson had fixed up a bunch of stuff inside. So despite the fact that it still looked derelict, it was in better shape than it had been before.

The blackened remains of the barn were off to the right, along with the other outbuildings, which were in worse shape than the house.

I wasn't going to lie—this hurt to see.

A knock came at my window. Violet had pulled up behind me. We'd agreed to meet here—me to finally get over avoiding seeing the place, Violet to check on the property, and both of us to get some footage for a social media scheme she'd cooked up.

I sucked in a breath, pushed back my shoulders, and stepped out of the car.

"Cookie?" Violet said, holding out a little plastic bag filled with what looked like homemade chocolate chip cookies.

I grinned as I took one. "Mrs. Foley found you?"

"Right outside Marybeth's shop. She said I deserved cookies for, how did she put it? 'All the stress that comes with my job and a new marriage.' She also gave us a pretty little knick-knack as a wedding gift. And that was after Marybeth came outside and apologized for her brother. I told her he didn't do anything wrong, which I think she appreciated. And when I finally extracted myself from Mrs. Foley with the cookies, two other people stopped me and asked if we were really hoping to bring the ranch back and start a family here. I don't suppose you'd know anything about that?"

I bit down on the cookie to give myself a minute before answering. I probably should have told her about that yarn I'd spun for Mrs. Adams and Mrs. Garcia. "What did you say?" I asked after I swallowed.

"I gave them my most convincing smile and said of course. And then I told them how devastated we were that the land was being taken for an amusement park, which didn't fit the character of this town at all."

I brushed the cookie crumbs off my hands and laughed. "You think just like me."

She grinned. "I figured that's what you would have told them."

"It slipped my mind to tell you that I started that particular rumor. But thank you for keeping it up. Now . . ." I glanced around. "Should we take a stroll around our future children's home?"

She smacked my arm with the bag of cookies. I swiped the bag and held it over my head as she reached for it.

"She gave those cookies to *me*, Ward. I'm the one who looked like she needed cookies, not you." But she was laughing as she jumped up to try to get them back.

I lifted the bag higher and managed to pry a cookie out of it before I handed it back.

"Thief." She stuck her tongue out at me, and I laughed as I took a giant bite from the cookie.

"Come on," I said, holding out a hand. "Let's walk."

She hesitated, and just as I realized there was no reason for us to hold hands out here where no one could see, she wrapped her palm around mine.

I shouldn't let that happen—not after that scorching kiss at the Summer Carnival, and not after I'd told her that we needed to put some distance between us.

But I didn't let go. I didn't want to.

Instead, I pressed my fingertips to the back of her small hand and tried to pretend as if it didn't mean anything.

"Marybeth asked if I wanted to meet up with her and Larkin for dinner tomorrow," she said, her voice quiet as we walked around the house.

"That's good." Marybeth, Larkin, and Emily were all friends, and it was nice of Marybeth to want to include Violet. Even though it wouldn't be for long.

"Do you think she really wants to be my friend? Or does she feel like she's required to invite me?"

I pulled my gaze from the second-floor window that had been my room as a kid and glanced down at Violet. She was chewing on her lip and looking at the ground.

She was really worried about Marybeth liking her.

"Hey," I said, pausing as we rounded the corner of the house. When she didn't look up, I gently lifted her chin to look me in the eye. Then I dropped my hand before it wandered up of its own accord to cup her cheek. "From what my brothers say, Marybeth is one of the best people in this town. She was nice to me in high school, even though her brothers hated us. I don't think you have to worry about her having an agenda."

Violet nodded. "It's kind of my default, you know. Assuming everyone's working an angle."

I made a face, realizing I had the tendency to do the same. "Byproduct of our jobs," I said. "We wouldn't be any good at them if we weren't so cynical."

She gave a little laugh, and I smiled, trying not to remember that I actually *didn't* have a job at this moment in time.

"What about your friends back in Missoula?" I asked, realizing she'd never mentioned anyone she kept in touch with. "Did you feel that way with them?"

She shrugged. "Tell me about this place," she said, ignoring my question as we walked toward the outbuildings.

I looked at her a moment, but she gave nothing away. I supposed there was a reason she didn't want to talk about her friends, so I let it go. "There's not a lot to tell. It was a good ranch, one of the best around, Pops always said. I don't know if that was true or him bragging, but I always wanted to believe it."

"It's big," she said, lifting a hand to shield her eyes from the lowering sun. "I don't remember the exact acreage, but I've got it somewhere in my files."

"It wasn't always as big as it is now. Pops bought several acres here and there when the money started coming in." I frowned and looked away from Violet, hoping she wouldn't ask about the money. It was an ugly part of our family history, one I'd done my best to steer clear of as Jackson, and even Nick for a little while, hurled themselves into it. I'd put all my energy into the legitimate ranch work and into school, making myself too busy for anything else.

"He bought more land?" Violet was looking up at me, clearly curious.

"Yeah. I thought you would've seen that in the deeds?"

"I didn't do the research myself. I had Kyle Clemmons pull all of that, and I was really only interested in making sure there weren't any outstanding liens that might tie everything up."

"It was a long time ago. He bought from neighbors on both sides, a few acres each. He even bought some acreage off Carson Noble, can you believe that?"

"Really? That's surprising," Violet said. "When was that?"

"There was a drought when I was a kid, and Noble fell on hard times. Pops told me about all the land he'd bought back then." He'd told me more, details that I wasn't sure Violet really wanted to hear about. As soon as he bought that land, he got busy building the warehouse at the far edge of the property. He needed that because he'd done more than buy land from Noble.

He'd also stolen a good chunk of Carson Noble's drug smuggling business. Kicked the man when he was down and built his own empire. I never could decide if I admired the business acumen or wished it had never happened.

Sometimes I wished I wasn't the one he'd confided in.

"If only the barn was still standing," Violet said, as we stopped at the remnants of it.

I kicked at a charred piece of wood. It fell apart immediately. "Yeah. Did you look into pressing charges for that?" Normally I was all about keeping the peace with this family loyalty nonsense, but it pissed me off that Drake Noble basically admitted to Marybeth that he'd set the fire, and then he'd scampered back to Florida, getting away with it.

She shook her head. "Not worth it. And honestly, I'd learned enough about the family politics in this town to realize I wanted to keep the company neutral."

I couldn't help but laugh. "And now you've married into it."

She let out a laugh too. "I guess I did." She was quiet a moment, letting her gaze rove over the house, the giant evergreen the driveway curved around, the too-long grasses waving in the breeze.

"Why is Chestnut Moon buying up so much land around here?" I asked, unable to hold back the curiosity any longer.

She shrugged. "We can get it cheap. I don't know, honestly. They don't really tell me why they want things done. I just do them." She paused, a smile lifting the corners of her mouth as she looked from the house to me. "It's so peaceful out here. What was it like here when you were a kid?"

"Loud," I said immediately. "Nothing like this. Between the cattle and the equipment and the ranch hands and all us kids, it was only quiet in the dead of night."

She smiled a little, like she was trying to picture it. "I can almost see bikes lying in the front yard and muddy footprints up the porch steps."

Nostalgia washed over me. "My stepmom used to decorate that tree for Christmas." I nodded at the big evergreen.

"I'd decorate the porch too. String some lights over the railing and along the top," Violet said with a faraway look in her eyes. "I always wanted a house to decorate."

I watched her a moment, and then followed her gaze toward the house, imagining it lit up with warmth and light. And for half a second, I could see myself at the window, arms wrapped around Violet.

I shook my head to clear it as Violet pointed to the porch. "That's a good spot, don't you think?"

I might have groaned a little. "I was hoping you'd forget about that."

Violet grinned and pulled out her phone. "I'd never forget one of my brilliant ideas."

"*Brilliant*," I said with a laugh. "You aren't suffering from low self-esteem, are you?"

"Nope. And neither are you. Go stand there." She gestured at the railing of the porch.

"In front of it or behind?"

"Hmm." She frowned, considering. "Let's start with in front. I think the light will be better."

By the time I'd reached the railing, she'd pulled a tripod from her car and was setting it up.

"Seriously?" I said as I leaned against the porch railing.

"It has to look good. People will scroll right past bad pictures." She messed with the tripod, and just as I was sure the sun would set before she was ready, Violet jogged to my side.

"Okay," she said. "Just go with it."

"Go with—"

She'd grabbed hold of my collar and yanked me down to meet her lips, the rest of my question dying against a furious kiss.

"Perfect," she said, smiling up at me after she cut it off much too soon.

"Really? Because I thought it could be longer."

She tapped her fingers against my cheek before letting go. "Those are still photos. No one can tell the passage of time. Besides, weren't you the one who said we needed to be careful?"

Heat flamed in my cheeks, and I rubbed a hand against the back of my neck. She was right.

Why exactly had I said that again?

"This time, we'll just look into each other's eyes, like we're picturing our whole lives here together, on this ranch," Violet said as she ran to set the timer on her phone again.

When she scampered back, I took her into my arms, looked down, and tried really hard not to laugh. Her teeth bit into her lip as she held back giggles. Somehow, we made it through several seconds like that as her phone snapped picture after picture.

We were partway through a video clip of us dancing on the porch when a truck pulled into the driveway.

Chapter Twenty-three

Violet

Ward twirled me back toward him. I'd just landed safely in his arms, the video still running, when he froze.

"Someone's here," he said as the sound of tires crunching over gravel drowned out the buzz of bees and birdsong.

I stayed where I was, in his arms, as we studied the truck. The setting sun hit the windshield hard enough that I couldn't see who was inside.

Then the driver's side door opened, and out stepped Luke Noble. Behind me, Ward stiffened.

Did Luke know what had happened between Ward and Wilder last night? I hoped not. Although with the way word traveled in a small town like this, it seemed unlikely.

Another man, one I hadn't seen before, stepped out of the passenger side door. He wore glasses and pants that actually had creases pressed into them.

"He's not from around here," I whispered to Ward.

"What do they want?" An uncharacteristic irritation sat on the edge of his words.

Maybe Ward had been enjoying our photo shoot as much as I had. I tamped down that thought and focused on the men in the driveway.

"Good evening!" the nicely dressed man said. He took a few steps closer to us, and I could tell he was closer to middle aged.

"Evening," Ward said carefully. He reached for my hand and led me to the porch steps, where I stopped the video filming. "Is there something we can help you with?" He directed the question at the stranger, but it was clear he really meant it for Luke.

Luke leaned against the front fender of his truck. "Harker. Miss Barnes." He nodded toward me. "My apologies. *Mrs.* Harker."

I didn't know how he could make a name sound so ugly. I pressed my free hand against my leg to steady my thoughts. "No apology needed, Luke. I kept my name."

His eyes flicked to Ward and back to me, a knowing sort of smile crossing his lips.

"Violet and I were enjoying our evening out here before you arrived. You care to tell us what it is you want?" Ward said evenly. Every hint of annoyance or anger was perfectly tucked away. His fingers twined in between mine, reminding me that we were in this together.

"I'm sorry for the interruption," the older man said. "I'm Phil Larson with Interstate Amusements." He stepped forward and held out a hand.

It took less than a second for me to realize this man worked for the company that wanted to develop the amusement park, and I knew Ward had pieced it together too by the way his fingers tightened around mine.

But nothing showed on his face, and he actually stepped forward and shook the man's hand. Gritting my teeth, I dropped Ward's grasp and did the same.

"Ward Harker," he said. "This is my wife, Violet Barnes."

"Ah, yes." Phil's pleasant smile went a little colder. "You work for the investment firm that's actually against progress."

I raised my eyebrows. "The only thing my company is against is actions that aren't in its best interest."

"Spoken like a true soldier." Phil laughed, and it grated on every nerve in my body.

How dare he insinuate that I was nothing but a mouthpiece for Chestnut Moon? He didn't know the first thing about me.

He had *no* idea that if it weren't for my family, I'd run as far away as I could from my job.

I almost choked on that realization. Instead I covered my mouth and coughed.

"Why are you here?" Ward's gaze slid from Phil to where Luke still leaned against the truck, arms crossed.

"Phil was in town and wanted to scope out the place in person. You know, since he'll be buying it from the county soon," Luke said. He pointed at the house. "You ought to put a big coaster right there. Or maybe an ice cream stand. Everyone likes ice cream on a hot day."

Ward went rigid beside me, and I reached for his hand again.

"This isn't a good time," I said, my words as cold as the ice cream Luke dreamed up. "You need to call our attorney if you want to see the place."

Luke shrugged. "You didn't look all that busy. Just prancing in front of a camera."

"They're called wedding photos," I shot back at him. "It might be a foreign concept to you, Luke Noble, but some of us enjoy being in love and like to capture memories of it."

His cool demeanor fell immediately, as if I'd aimed an arrow right at his heart. It almost looked like he was in pain, the way he frowned and then quickly turned around.

I didn't know what I'd done, but Luke gripped the door handle of his truck, held his hand there for a second, and then yanked it open. "Let's go, Larson."

Phil appeared surprised at the turn of events, but he didn't argue.

"Call our lawyer next time," I called after him as he returned to the passenger side.

"Else we'll consider it trespassing," Ward added.

Luke finally looked up, his hand curled around the edge of the truck door. He looked right past me to Ward. "You've got nothing here. None of you. And you bet I'm going to enjoy every second of taking this last little shred of your claim here away. Everything will be back to the way it was, minus the Harkers." His eyes flicked back to me. "Feel free to pass that on to those suits you work for. They picked the losing side."

He turned around in the driveway, wheels kicking up gravel. Neither Ward nor I said a word until the last sound from the truck died in the dusk around us.

"What did I say to him that . . . that . . ." I couldn't even put words to the way Luke had looked.

Ward pulled my phone from the tripod and handed it to me. I shoved it into my pocket.

"He lost his wife," Ward finally said. "Bad car accident, according to what I've heard."

"Oh." I pressed a hand to my heart. I wanted to put the man in his place, not throw a personal tragedy in his face. "I wish I hadn't said that."

"Well," Ward said, folding up the tripod and handing to me. "It got them off the property, didn't it?"

"I still feel bad about it. That's not how I operate."

He wrapped an arm around my shoulders and pulled me closer. "I know it isn't. You didn't know. How could you?"

I shrugged, still feeling guilty.

"Hey," he said, resting his chin on my head. "Were those really wedding photos?"

I laughed a little. "I mean, I guess they could be. That's a good angle for posting them, actually."

"All right, just promise me one thing."

I looked up at him. "What's that?"

"Don't post any where I look like this." He widened his eyes and made the most ridiculous-looking face I'd ever seen.

I laughed and tapped him on the chest. "Of course not. I'm saving that one for the Christmas card."

Chapter Twenty-four

Marybeth

"Thank you *so* much for coming over here instead of going out," Larkin said when Violet and I arrived at her door with bags of take-out from the tiny Chinese place near the interstate. "My mom just took off to work the night shift at the hospital, and Diego's already in bed."

"Of course." I set my bags on the kitchen counter as Emily appeared behind Larkin. "Can we freak out again about how you're actually engaged?"

Larkin laughed, and her face went pink as she looked at the ring again. "Do you want to know what's really crazy? Nick kept suggesting spring or summer next year for a wedding date so I'd have plenty of time to plan, but I don't think I want to wait that long."

I grinned. "I can't imagine him being mad at that. After all, he was the one so eager to get married."

"You can definitely get married fast at the courthouse, if you want to," Violet said as she took the containers out of the bag. She looked up and made a face. "I wouldn't call it romantic, though."

I looked at Larkin, who was trying so hard not to laugh. But she didn't have to, since Violet started laughing first.

"I'm sorry," Violet said, waving a hand as if she were fanning her face. "I couldn't resist."

I nodded, feeling a little guilty. I hadn't really thought much about Violet as a person before talking to her outside the library that day. She'd always just been the face of a soulless corporation. It was nice to see another side of her.

Larkin grabbed some plates and forks, while Emily found a bottle of wine, and we carried the food to the small dining table.

I piled some pork fried rice onto my place and grabbed an eggroll as the others chatted about the food, and I thought about the conversation Emily and I had on the way to Luke's a while back. How much would it take before I'd ever agree to do what Violet had done? I was dying to know what the motivation had been for her. A promotion? A giant bonus? Ownership in the company? Maybe they bought her a house or a car.

Finally, I couldn't stand the curiosity any more.

"Okay," I said to Violet. "You have to tell me what you're getting out of this arrangement with Ward. The curiosity is killing me."

She took a drink of her wine before answering. "I thought he would've told you. My company wants to keep that property, and they figured we'd have a better chance at swaying the town's opinion of us if I became one of you."

"Not that. I know what Chestnut Moon wants. I meant *you*. Why would you agree to that? It's kind of a big deal to get married. No one really ever plans to do it more than once."

"Oh, that." Her face remained impassive, but her cheeks colored just slightly. And I had the weirdest feeling that maybe Violet Barnes didn't really mind being married to Ward Harker.

Which was crazy . . . but stranger things had happened in this town. Like me and Gabe.

"What do you get out of it?" Larkin asked, clearly curious now too. "Are they paying you a bunch of money?"

She shrugged again, but it was less sure this time. "In a way. Yes."

I glanced at Larkin before turning back to Violet. Something about this felt off. "Are they blackmailing you or something?"

"Oh, no," she said with a nervous laugh as she reached for an egg roll. "Nothing like that. Just . . . I mean, I guess it's not a secret or anything. Just embarrassing, so I don't really talk about it. They've helped out with my family, paying for stuff. My dad's been sick." Her words were halting, as if we were the first people she'd ever told any of this to.

I frowned and leaned back in the chair. "So it's like you're paying them back? That's a weird way to repay someone." Not that I wanted her to run off and divorce Ward right this second, but it was strange, and I felt like she needed someone to say that.

"More or less." She paused. "If you don't mind, can you not mention this to anyone else? Ward already suspects I'm having trouble with money. If he knew about the situation with my family, he'd want to help."

"And you don't want that," Larkin finished for her. "I get it. If this was a real relationship, I'd tell you to be honest with him. But since it's not, a little white lie can't hurt."

That made Violet go even pinker, and she ducked her head.

"You know who I think is having money trouble?" I said, thinking out loud as I dumped more sweet and sour sauce onto my plate. "My brother."

"Really?" Larkin tilted her head, noodles sliding off her fork as she studied me. "What makes you think that?"

"It's just a feeling I have. Emily, remember when we went over there to get the chickens?"

Emily nodded.

"I found out he'd only hired back about half the usual summer help. And then the other day, when I took Wilder home, he told me he sold this grandfather clock that had been in our family for generations."

"I remember that clock," Larkin said, laying her fork down. "Your mom is going to kill him when she finds out. No way would she agree to that."

"Tell me about it. Why would he do that if he wasn't hurting for money?"

"It makes sense." Violet leaned forward. "Remember I said there had to be something in this whole amusement park thing for Luke, beyond revenge?"

I nodded slowly. "But you know what doesn't make sense? I kept the books for the ranch for a while, and everything was fine then. It wasn't a gold mine, but he wasn't broke. That wasn't all that long ago. How could it have gotten so bad off since then?"

"Debt?" Violet suggested. "Did he buy anything big, or build anything?"

"I don't think so. Nothing I could see, anyway."

"Gambling?" Emily suggested.

I shook my head.

"Maybe it's just a downturn in the business," Violet said.

"That wouldn't just affect Luke. We'd have heard about it because it would've affected every rancher in the valley."

Violet nodded. "Well," she said after a while. "At least we know he isn't spending everything he has on cars. That truck he was in last night when he came by the property needed a bath, a new front bumper, and a fresh paint job."

I smiled, but pain twisted the good memories of that old truck. Luke had driven it for years, but I'd be surprised if he ever let me step foot inside it again.

"Wait, he came by the ranch?" Larkin asked. "Last night?"

Violet filled Larkin in on what I'd already heard from Gabe. We talked about it some more, and then the conversation drifted to other things—Diego's new favorite cartoon (which drove Larkin crazy), my shop redecoration, and Emily's parents' upcoming trip to Hawaii. Violet stayed quiet as we talked.

Emily ducked out early. Larkin excused herself to check on Diego, while Violet and I cleaned up the dishes and leftover food.

"Is your dad going to be okay?" I asked her.

She hesitated, as if she didn't want to tell me. "I don't know. But Mom takes good care of him. She drives him crazy, always checking his temperature and making sure he takes his meds."

I smiled at that. "I'm glad they have each other. I hope everything works out."

"Thank you." Violet opened the fridge to put away the takeout containers. "You know," she said, clearly changing the subject. "As many times as I've been out to that property, it was like I was seeing it through completely new eyes last night. Did you know Ward's stepmom—I guess that's Gabe's mom?—used to decorate that giant tree out front for Christmas?"

I smiled. "Yeah. It's one of Gabe's favorite memories. I only ever saw it once or twice. We didn't really go by there very much when I was a kid. You know, the whole my dad hates your dad thing."

"It's weird that those properties share a boundary," Violet said, leaning against the countertop. "I'm kind of surprised you all weren't shooting each other over the top of the fence."

I grimaced. For all I knew, it did happen. I'd learned more about my family's past in the last few months than I'd ever known when I was growing up and it was actually happening. "That property line is way off in the far corner. You'd have to get on a four-wheeler or a horse unless you wanted a really long hike. It's a pretty short boundary too, from what I know. I doubt anyone really thought about it that much."

Violet looked confused. "But Ward's father bought some of your family's land, didn't he? Several years ago?"

I shook my head. "I don't think so. But honestly, I don't know. I wasn't exactly into the ranch when I was younger, except for my chickens and riding the horses."

"That's what Ward told me." Violet poured another glass of wine and held up the bottle in a question.

I pushed my empty glass across the countertop. "That's interesting. Gabe never mentioned it."

"Probably not a big deal," she replied, setting the bottle down. "He didn't say how much. It might've only been a few acres. Apparently there was a drought and the Harkers bought a lot of land off of neighbors."

I nodded slowly. I remembered the drought. It stressed my parents out, and even as a kid, I'd known better during that time than to ask for new toys or anything that wasn't necessary.

"So," Larkin said as she came back into the kitchen. "Tell me exactly how annoying it is to live with Ward."

She looked so serious that I almost spat out my wine as I laughed.

"He's not annoying," Violet said.

"Please." Larkin rolled her eyes. "All that bravado. He's like a character in a Hallmark movie. The self-important CEO who thinks he knows everything and spends his free time squashing cute little mom-and-pop businesses."

I was laughing so hard that I had to put my wine down.

"I don't mean it in a bad way," Larkin said as she grinned. "He's just really different from his brothers."

"You mean smarter?" Violet said. "Also better looking."

I raised my eyebrows as I lifted the glass to my mouth again. Maybe I wasn't so off base earlier.

"Hmm," Larkin said, exchanging a glance with me.

"Oh, please," Violet said. "He's not so bad."

"Hmm," I repeated with a half-smile at Violet.

"Really! He's kind of a nice guy."

"Kind of," I said, waggling my eyebrows at Larkin.

"I *kind of* get the feeling that you don't mind having him around every day," Larkin said.

"Stop," Violet replied, but her usual nonplussed expression had vanished more and more with each sip of wine. Her face went red as a smile crept across her lips.

I grinned at Larkin, who then pressed for more details from Violet. She remained tight-lipped, even though it was obvious now that something was going on between her and Ward.

I finished off my wine and washed the glass out in the sink, thinking back to Violet's revelation about Mr. Harker buying land off my dad.

And something clicked as I set the glass down on the drying rack.

Maybe Luke wasn't hurting for money.

Maybe he was *saving* it.

Chapter Twenty-five

Ward

I tossed the ball to Barker, who caught it and promptly ran off to a far corner of Gabe and Marybeth's backyard.

"Our dog is bad at playing fetch," I called to Violet, who was examining the flowers Marybeth had in planters on the back porch. *Our* dog. It felt so natural coming out of my mouth that I'd barely noticed what I was saying.

"Well, at least she isn't staring at the chickens anymore." Violet gestured at the well-protected coop, filled with chickens who let us know exactly how they felt about us borrowing the yard for Barker.

"True." I glanced toward the tree where Barker had parked herself, chin laying protectively on the ball. "Do you think she'll ever bring it back?"

Violet studied the dog. "When she gets bored." She paused. "Hey, Ward?"

"Mmm?"

"What's going to happen to Barker when . . . you know . . ."

My insides constricted at the unfinished question. I looked over at her. Her hair hung straight today, and I liked the way it framed her profile. I tried to imagine what it would be like to wake up and not have her next to me, with Barker shoved between us.

And I couldn't.

I swallowed. "I don't know."

She looked up at me then. Her mouth opened, and then closed again. The silence stretched between us as birds twittered in a nearby tree and leaves rustled in the breeze. It felt like someone should say something, but at the same time, I knew if either one of us did, it would be an acknowledgment that this wasn't going to last forever.

Violet's phone buzzed, and I finally let out a breath.

"There's another town meeting. Tuesday night," she said, her eyes on the phone screen.

"Is that your boss?" I asked.

She nodded. "Apparently Phil Larson wants to speak to the council."

I scowled. "They're already on his side. What else does he want?"

"Not necessarily." Violet slipped her phone back into her pocket. "After all, he hasn't been here. Volunteering, and talking to people, and being a part of this town."

She was right. "Maybe it's worked better than we thought."

"He could be afraid," Violet said. "I'm sure Luke's kept him informed. Maybe this is a last-ditch effort to keep the town on his side. If that's the case, then we need to do something."

We were quiet a moment. Possibilities shot through my mind, one after the other as I discarded them. Only one made sense, but I didn't dare bring it up. Not again.

Not when it felt too close to the truth.

"What if we . . ." Violet started, her eyes on Barker. "I mean, we put those pictures on social media, and you told those ladies about how . . ."

I couldn't take my eyes off her now, and slowly, she turned to look at me.

The words were on the tip of my tongue. I either said them out loud or we danced around this again. I never minced words in the boardroom. It was time to do the same here. "About how we wanted to start our lives together on the ranch?"

She swallowed visibly. "Yes." She didn't have to finish her thoughts. *What if we stood up and said that out loud to everyone?*

I wanted to reach for her. To take her hand, to pull her close to me. But I didn't dare. Not yet. I wanted the truth without any persuasion involved. "Vi?"

She tilted her head.

"What do you think about me?"

Her eyebrows lifted slightly, as if that wasn't the question she expected. And maybe it wasn't, but it was something I needed answered.

She studied me a moment. "I think—no, I *know* there's a lot more to you than you want anyone to believe there is. Anyone can see that you're smart and you're driven—I shouldn't even be telling you that because it's going to inflate your already enormous ego." She grinned.

"Go on," I said, smiling back at her.

Violet shook her head. "Not a chance. I'm going to tell you things that I don't think you want to believe. Like how much you love being with your family. And how much you love this town. And how you're missing some big piece of who you really are out in California, and that since you've been here, you've started to realize that too."

I clenched my jaw. Violet didn't pull any punches, and I should've known she'd seen right through the façade I'd fought to keep up. "Why would I care about a place that destroyed my family?"

"I don't know," she said softly. "I can't answer that for you. But you do. I can see it when you talk to people, and in how you spoke about the traditions here, and in the look in your eyes at the old ranch. You care a lot, Ward. Whether you want to or not."

Barker chose that moment to arrive back at my feet, ball in her mouth. I tossed it toward the far side of the yard and she took off.

Violet was still watching me. "I understand if you don't want to stay here, you know. If you'd rather go back to LA."

There was a question underlying that comment. I could hear it clear as day, and when I caught her gaze, it was there too, lingering in the warm brown of her eyes. She was ready to put herself out there.

Was I?

I sucked in a breath. *Tell the truth.* "I don't know. You're right about Bent Creek. Maybe I can be here. Maybe not. It's been mostly okay, surprisingly."

"*Okay?*" she repeated, her voice a little flat.

I'd said the wrong thing. Caution be damned, I was putting myself out there now. I reached for her hand, and after half a second of reticence, she let me take it. "I was talking about the town. Not you."

She didn't say anything—just waited for me to continue.

I ran a hand over my face, feeling ten kinds of awkward all of a sudden. "You caught me by surprise, Vi," I finally said. "I don't hate what we have."

"Oh wow, you're terrible at this." She covered her mouth, and I was pretty sure she was trying not to laugh.

I squeezed my eyes shut and opened them again. "Let me try again. I'll go simple this time. You're smart. You're gorgeous. You're crazy good at your job. You're funny. I like spending time with you. I want us to keep our dog. Can I kiss you now?"

Instead of responding, she rose onto her toes, reached for the back of my head, and pulled my face down to meet hers. As I wound my fingers through her hair, all I could think was that even if we lost everything here in Bent Creek, I'd still come out a winner.

Chapter Twenty-six

Marybeth

I was pulling a garland off a snow-themed tree when Wilder wandered into my shop.

He paused about five steps in, his eyes going wide. "This is something else."

I wound the garland around the length of my arm, smiling as I walked toward him. He still looked disheveled, but at least he appeared to be sober. That was an improvement. "Thanks, I think."

"How many trees have you got in here?" His gaze roved the store, and I imagined he was trying to count.

"I don't remember," I said honestly. "I keep adding new ones."

"You always were obsessed with Christmas. I guess I shouldn't be surprised that you're selling it now."

I set the garland on the countertop above the register. "Want some peppermint hot chocolate?"

"In the summer?"

"Why not?"

He shrugged. "Sure."

I busied myself with ladling out the hot chocolate and dropping in mini marshmallows, trying to figure out why he'd come in here. He hadn't reached out at all since I'd rescued him outside the bar and brought him home.

"What's with the summer stuff?" he asked.

I turned around and handed him the mug as he examined the display that now took up half the front window. "A ploy to draw in more customers. Summer visitors are looking for sunglasses, bug spray, insulated water bottles, stuff like that. I've been hooking them in with that, and then some of them go on to buy an ornament or something too."

Wilder nodded and took a sip of the hot chocolate. "That's smart. And this is really good."

"Thanks." I straightened a couple of the sunglasses on their display. "So . . . did you decide you just had to come visit me?"

He gave me a sheepish half smile. "Something like that." He glanced down at his mug for a moment before looking back up at me. "I owe you a thanks and an apology."

I waved a hand at him, like he didn't need to do that. But at the same time, it felt good to know that at least one of my brothers appreciated me.

"I was in a bad way when you found me. I found out about Makayla, and I had to get out. I jumped on the next plane headed this way. I broke up with her in a text." He winced at the thought.

"Ouch." Although if what he said about her was true, I didn't know if she deserved better.

"I just didn't want to hear any excuses, you know? I didn't want to hear her voice." He swallowed, then immediately took another sip of the hot chocolate.

I nodded in empathy. He looked so lost that I had to reach out and squeeze his arm. "I'm sorry."

"Thanks." He heaved a sigh. "And thank you for dragging my sorry ass home. You shouldn't have had to do that."

I wrapped my arms around myself, not wanting to let on how hard it was to show up at the ranch with Luke waiting there with all his condescension. "I wasn't just going to leave you on the street like that."

"And then the Summer Carnival, and . . ." He rubbed his forehead. "I'm sorry. I'm a walking disaster right now."

"You're upset. It's a normal reaction. Maybe just lay off the drinking for now, okay?" I suggested gently.

He nodded. "Yeah, I got that part figured out, at least. Can you tell your friend I'm sorry? For whatever I did at the Summer Carnival."

"For what it's worth, she said all you did was tell her all about Makayla. But I'll pass it on to her."

"Thanks. I've got enough going on without worrying about Ward Harker jumping me outside the diner one night." He gave a short laugh. "Who would've ever thought? That kid was all talk and no action in high school. He'd piss you off and then immediately talk you out of hitting him."

I grinned. "Did you know he convinced our algebra teacher that last period was canceled one day?"

"Not surprised." Wilder laughed before growing more serious. "Watch yourself around him, okay?"

I raised my eyebrows. "Is this where you do Luke's bidding and tell me I'm a traitor and that I'm throwing my life away?"

"Whoa." He held up a hand. "Not what I said."

I immediately felt bad. It was Luke who'd driven this wedge between us, not Wilder. "Sorry. I just figured that you and Luke were on the same page."

He said nothing. Instead, he finished off his hot chocolate and carried the empty mug over to the counter, leaving me to wonder where exactly he stood.

"Look," he said, leaning against the counter. "I'm not going to pretend I love what's going on here, because I don't. Would I rather you find someone else? Yes. But am I going to punish you for it? No."

He sounded so much like his twin at that moment that it was uncanny. "That's pretty much what Drake said to me a few months ago when he was here."

"Big surprise, us thinking alike," Wilder said with a grin.

I smiled back, just grateful to have him here. Despite everything, I missed my brothers and my parents something awful. "I'm glad you came home. I miss everyone so much. How're Mom and Dad?"

"Good. The doctor told Dad his blood pressure was too high, and now Mom's watching everything he eats like a hawk."

"I bet he hates that," I said as I rearranged the summer-themed children's books I had on display next to the sunhats and SPF 35. "Violet's dad is sick, and she was telling me how her mom is always checking his temperature. It drives him crazy."

Wilder winced at the mention of Violet. "Don't forget to tell Violet I said sorry, okay?"

"I will. I promise. She's got a lot on her mind, with her dad and the finances. She probably hasn't given it a second thought."

"Maybe," Wilder said as he straightened.

I brushed my hands together, admiring my work. "Hey," I said, an idea blossoming in my mind. "Are you going back to the ranch?"

"Planned on it. Luke's ready to put me to work, unfortunately."

I pressed my lips together, thinking this was maybe too much to ask. But I didn't have anything to lose. "Has he mentioned saving money for anything?"

Wilder held my gaze. "What do you mean?"

He knew something. That much was evident in how carefully he looked at me. "Nothing," I said slowly. "Just that he's hurting for help out there, and then he told me he sold that old grandfather clock."

"That's something you'll have to talk to him about," Wilder replied. "It's his place now, not mine."

"Right." I shook off the uncomfortable feeling that Wilder was keeping something from me. If anything, it confirmed my suspicions. "See you soon?"

He gave me a genuine smile. "You bet."

And then he headed out the door, back to the ranch and the brother I was almost certain would be getting a good deal on some acreage once Summit County sold the old Harker ranch to Interstate Amusements.

Chapter Twenty-seven

Violet

I knew something was wrong the second I stepped onto Main Street Saturday morning.

No one waved at me or said hello. Instead, they darted furtive glances my way. And I could have sworn that even nice old Mrs. Young, who worked part time at the diner and always offered me extra soup, actually frowned at me.

I thought about texting Ward, but it felt crazy. What would I say? *People are looking at me weird on the street.* Instead, I slipped inside the welcoming door of Mountain Roasters, grateful to see Larkin behind the counter.

Only one person was in the coffee shop, and he left after looking down his nose at me.

I hurried toward Larkin. "Okay, maybe I'm losing my mind, but I feel like something is going on."

Larkin's expression confirmed it before she said anything at all.

"What?" I asked as she reached for an empty cup.

"It's bad." She set the cup on the counter.

My heart lurched into my stomach. I wished I'd opted for coffee instead of orange juice at breakfast this morning, although I had the feeling that no amount of coffee would help me deal with whatever it was Larkin was about to share with me.

As if she was reading my mind, Larkin got the coffeepot and poured before she started speaking. She set the pot down and turned back toward me, pushing a pitcher of creamer across the counter. "Remember what you told us the other night? When we had Chinese over at my place?"

"About Ward?" My face went hot just thinking about admitting that I had feelings for him.

"Not that. About your dad. And the money."

"The money," I repeated, running the conversation through my head again.

"That Chestnut Moon was helping with some expenses for your family." Larkin leaned on the counter with her elbows.

I nodded slowly. "Okay. But I only shared that with you guys." I'd never told another soul about that.

She rubbed her face, and my heart sunk. She'd said it was bad. What else could there be?

"So apparently, word got out about that. I don't know how. But then it got twisted somehow, and now people are saying that you and Ward are only fighting the amusement park idea because you were promised a big payday from Chestnut Moon."

"What?" I gaped at her. "I mean, yes, I get paid for my job. But that's it. There's nothing extra. I haven't even asked them to help out with the bills recently. The last thing they paid were taxes on Mom and Dad's house." Which I wished I'd never asked them to cover at all.

"I don't know what happened. But someone went digging, and they claim that you're basically broke. That you're losing your apartment, and that Ward's lost his job, and you're both in really bad financial situations. That Chestnut Moon is covering your parents' bills. And that if you're successful with stopping the amusement park, they've promised you both tons of money."

I gripped the cup of coffee in my hands, hardly understanding what Larkin was saying. "That doesn't make sense. Some of it's true, but not all of it. It's like someone took the truth and turned it sideways into something else completely. Who would do that?"

It was a dumb question with an obvious answer. Larkin tilted her head and raised her eyebrows.

"Luke Noble," I answered for myself. And then I felt sick. The only way he'd find out would be if one of us had told him. "But how . . .?" It wasn't me. I couldn't figure out why or how Larkin or Emily would have.

But Marybeth . . . She was his sister. "I trusted her," I whispered, staring at the smooth surface of my coffee.

"I don't know what happened," Larkin said. "I haven't talked to Marybeth yet, but I will. I've known her forever, and I just can't imagine her willingly sharing that with him, not when it would hurt you and Ward and Gabe and all of us."

I pressed a hand to my stomach, trying to keep the panic from rising. I had to do damage control. Not only with the town, but with Ward. I hadn't told him anything about Chestnut Moon helping me out. Or my apartment. Or my dad.

This was *so* bad.

I closed my eyes as the panic surged. Beyond Luke, I had to figure out if Mac knew about any of this. What was he going to say when he found out how messed up everything had become?

My phone rang just then. I was afraid to look at it, but I reluctantly took it from my purse. Mac's name and number flashed onto the screen. "It's work," I told Larkin with a furtive glance in her direction.

Sympathy clouded her features.

"I don't know what I'm going to tell them." But I couldn't ignore the call. If I let it go, Mac would get more and more irritated. It was better to get it over with, and then start mitigating the damage.

"Hey Mac," I said as I pressed the phone to my ear.

"Barnes." He was seething. I could almost picture the look on his face just through the tone of his voice. "What the hell going on down there?"

I didn't even know where to start. "Mac—"

"I got this email—I don't know who it's from. It says you're running around with Ward Harker, bragging about taking us for—what was it? 'Millions,' it says. Millions of dollars."

"That's not true," I managed to say.

"If it's not, then you've made some serious enemies. You're supposed to be making friends. Wooing that town over to our side. *Stopping* this ridiculous eminent domain thing, not giving them fodder to push it forward. What are you doing? How are you going to fix this?"

"I'm already on it." My voice was barely a whisper. That wouldn't work. I felt like I was about to be sick, but the only way to impress Mac was to sound like I knew what I was doing. "I'll fix it. I promise," I said in a stronger voice.

"You'd better. I laid everything on the line for you, Barnes. I swore to the board that you could handle this. If you can't, you're done."

"I know," I said, closing my eyes and pressing the heel of my hand to my eyelids.

"*Fix* it. Now." And then he hung up.

"Are you okay?" Larkin asked after a moment.

I turned around to find her standing nearby. I started to nod, but really, I wasn't okay. Not at all. My reputation here was in tatters, and now I could lose my job over it.

Larkin squeezed my arm. "Go see Ward. He's probably heard about it by now. I'll talk to Marybeth and see if I can find out how this got out."

I nodded as I clutched my phone so hard I thought it would leave dents on my fingers. I didn't even remember I'd left my coffee behind until I was halfway back to the B&B. I avoided looking anyone in the eye, although I felt them all watching me. Probably thinking that I was a horrible person, who was just here to use them for money.

Nothing could be further from the truth.

I hugged myself as I approached the B&B. I *liked* this place. I never thought I'd feel that way when I first came here. But Bent Creek had worked its way into my heart, and the thought of not being wanted here anymore hurt so much that it was hard to breathe.

At least until I saw Ward waiting on the front porch of the B&B.

And I realized I had so much more to lose than a town.

Chapter Twenty-eight

Ward

For half a second, I forgot everything that Nick had just told me. When Violet looked up at me with worried brown eyes, all I wanted to do was open my arms and let her fall into them.

Until I remembered everything she'd kept from me. And how it was destroying everything my brothers had worked so hard for here.

"You know," I said in a voice I barely recognized. "I almost thought we could do it. That we could save the ranch. That it would be my family's again. That all the crap we went through here would finally be behind us because we actually *succeeded*." I gave a hollow laugh. "I was actually wondering what it might be like to stay here. Can you believe that?"

Those words barely scraped the surface. And they didn't even touch the part of me that hurt the most.

"Ward." Violet slowly climbed the stairs. When she reached the top, I took a step backward. I didn't trust myself to think straight if I got too close to her.

"I trusted you." I hated how incredulous I sounded. I felt turned inside out, incapable of sounding like my normal self. I'd lost control of everything, including my own reactions.

"It's a bunch of lies," she said, pain gleaming in her eyes.

I wanted to believe her. I wanted so badly to know she wasn't Parker. That she didn't just say things she didn't mean because it got her what she wanted. But I knew better. I might have gotten my heart broken, but I wasn't a fool. Not this time.

"So you aren't hurting for money?"

She closed her eyes a second and swallowed. "I am, kind of. But not—"

"You lost your apartment?"

"I didn't lose it. I gave it up."

"Because you're broke."

"Well . . ." She was searching for an answer.

"Why couldn't you be straight with me? I would've helped. I *asked* you if you needed help, more than once, and you said no."

"I barely knew you!" she shot back.

My blood boiled. "So instead of confiding in me and accepting my help, you took some deal with the devil. And now you're dragging me down with you."

"No!" She dropped her arms, her hands curling into fists at her sides. "That's not at all what happened."

"Then what did happen, Vi? Because from where I stand, all I see is someone who only cares about herself."

"It's not about me—"

I threw up my hands. "You getting a bunch of money if you made this happen *isn't* about you? What were you going to do, donate it to charity? Not that you have to worry about that now, because no one in their right mind is going to side with us after this."

"Will you *stop* interrupting me?" she yelled.

"I'm not—"

"*Stop!*"

I wrenched my mouth closed. Fine. If she wanted to spew lies at me, she could. I'd listen. And then I'd leave.

"First," she said, tapping one index finger against her palm. "There's no 'pile of money.' I married you because my boss threatened me both with losing my job and with the fact that they could take my parents' house if I didn't."

My insides crawled at her words. "Nice to know."

"Second, I'm not broke. I'm just . . . stretched thin because of my dad."

"Why? Did he steal from you?"

She closed her eyes, then opened them. "He's sick. Cancer."

It felt like she'd hurled a football at my stomach. "Also nice to know."

She seemed to curl in on herself. "Are you serious? I just told you my dad has cancer, and that's all you have to say?"

Was it possible to be angry and feel like an absolute jerk at the same time? "I didn't mean it that way. I'm sorry he's sick. But you could have told me weeks ago. You know, when I was telling you about losing my stepmom to cancer. Or when I was sharing my messed-up family history with you. Or when I told you about Parker. Any of those times I shared the hardest parts of my life with you, but you never reciprocated. I could've helped you, somehow. But you didn't trust me enough to tell me. How can I trust you if you don't trust me?"

She hugged herself around the middle. "I don't know what to say. I'm sorry I'm not as good at this as you are. I don't know why I can't talk about any of it, and . . . and maybe it's better if you don't put your trust in me."

With that, she pushed by me to the door.

That was it? She was *leaving*? "That's all you have to say?"

She looked back at me. "I'll talk to Mac. I'll figure this out."

The ice lacing her words strangled all the fire I had left.

I'd done it again. I found a woman who got me to care—to fall in love, if I was being honest—and then dropped me when she was done.

I sucked in a shaking breath. For someone who was so damn good at making deals, I was so incredibly bad at choosing women.

Chapter Twenty-nine

Marybeth

B efore I could answer the text from Larkin, my phone rang.

"What happened?" were the first words out of her mouth.

I paused, letting the ladder I'd just closed up lean against the wall of the shop. "What do you mean?"

"Violet and Ward? The scandal the entire town is talking about?" She was a little out of breath as she spoke, and I pictured her running across the coffee shop, delivering someone's latte as she was talking. Which was something Charlie Gates, the owner of Mountain Roasters, would hate but would never bring up to her because he was afraid of hearing from Nick.

I turned around, surveying my empty shop. "What do you mean? I've been here since seven o'clock." I was determined to make a lot of progress on this redecoration today.

"Someone let the entire town think that both Violet and Ward are only in this for the money. That he's lost his job and she's completely broke, and if they succeed in stopping the amusement park, they'll both walk away with millions. And, oh yeah, her dad is really sick, Chestnut Moon is keeping her family afloat, and she's lost her apartment."

My heart lurched, and I gripped the phone so hard I thought it might break. There was a kernel of truth in there. A truth that Violet had told us in confidence.

"Marybeth?" Larkin's voice echoed through the phone when I didn't say anything.

"I'm here," I said, pressing a hand to my forehead and trying to imagine the effect this story was having on the plan to stop the eminent domain action. "How bad is it?"

I could almost hear the lines forming in Larkin's face as she frowned. "It's not good. I haven't talked to Nick yet. Violet was here, and she . . . wasn't okay. Her boss called and tore into her, and she left to go find Ward."

"Okay," I said, my head a mess of thoughts.

"You know who did this." It wasn't a question, because I did know.

"Luke," I whispered. I felt sick. What had happened? Violet had confided in us about her family, and how Chestnut Moon had helped them, and how her job would've been on the line if she hadn't agreed to marry Ward. Besides Larkin and Emily—neither of whom would have told anyone—who else would have—?

My eyes widened.

Wilder.

"How did that happen? How did Luke find out?" Larkin spoke carefully, not accusing me, but wary.

"I didn't . . ." What had I said to Wilder? What was I *thinking*? It hadn't even occurred to me that he'd repeat any of our conversation.

Stupid. I was so stupid. I'd fallen for his sad story, tried to comfort him, and . . . Was it *all* a lie?

"Marybeth? Are you okay?" Larkin asked.

"No," I managed to say. "I'm going to see my brother."

Before Larkin could say anything else, I hung up and ran to grab my purse. My phone buzzed as I locked the door to Bent Creek Christmas. It was a text from Gabe.

My stomach swirled as I opened it up.

Call me.

I couldn't. Not now. If I heard the accusation in his voice, I wouldn't be able to do anything but curl into a ball in the corner and cry.

Instead, I hurried to my car, avoiding eye contact with anyone on the street. I probably looked crazy, especially since I wasn't the one who was the topic of gossip. But I didn't care.

I'd messed up. And I had to fix it, somehow.

My phone rang as I started the Honda. Gabe again. My finger hovered over the *Answer* button on the screen in my car, but I couldn't. Not until I'd done something.

What that something was, I didn't know yet.

Even when I pulled into the driveway at the ranch, I didn't know why I was there. What was I going to say? *Hey, Wilder, have you been lying to me the whole time you've been here?*

If I ran into Luke, I *really* didn't know what I was going to say.

I pressed my hands against the steering wheel, second-guessing everything. My phone buzzed again, and then a second time.

Reluctantly, I picked it up from the passenger seat. It was Gabe.

I'm at the shop. Where are you?

I'm getting worried. Call me.

Another buzz, and another text popped up. *I can't believe you're MIA right now.*

I squeezed my eyes shut with the awful feeling that Gabe thought I'd done this on purpose. I couldn't leave him hanging, but if I tried to talk to him right now, I'd break down.

I quickly tapped out a message. *Working on it. Will call you later.* I sent it and immediately turned off my phone. I couldn't handle the barrage of texts I knew I'd get.

Taking a ragged breath, I forced myself to focus on where I was—and to try to figure out what I was going to do. I spotted Luke's truck, a smattering of vehicles that belonged to the ranch hands, and the rental Wilder was driving. It was late morning, but not late enough for lunch yet.

With any luck, Wilder would be here and Luke wouldn't.

I forced myself out of the SUV. I knocked on the door of the house I'd lived in for most of my life and waited.

The seconds ticked by. I tried to think about anything other than what I would say to my brother. The breeze was warm, and it smelled the same as it always had. A mixture of wildflowers, straw, and manure, which was somehow reassuring. The trees were bright green, and the mountains soared in the distance, little caps of snow still on the peaks of the tallest ones. The rosebushes Mom had planted two decades ago were budding, and all I could think of was how incredibly beautiful this place was.

Sometimes, like now, I missed it so deeply that the ache was almost physically painful.

I knocked again. No answer.

Wilder had mentioned that Luke wanted to put him to work. Maybe that's where he was. It was probably best for him to stay busy, if he really had been dumped. I didn't know what to believe anymore.

Almost without thinking, I lifted the lid of the old charcoal grill that sat nearby. The silver key was still there, gleaming in the sunlight.

I hesitated only a second, then picked it up and fitted it into the lock. The door swung open to a silent house. I slipped the key into my pocket and stepped inside, closing the door behind me.

Light streamed through the windows in the kitchen, and the clock on the microwave flashed 12:00. I was the one who fixed stuff like that. Luke probably hadn't even noticed it needed to be reset.

My eyes traveled the length of the kitchen before I moved to the living room. The space where the grandfather clock had been was glaringly empty. I hoped Luke had gotten an earful from Mom on that.

I knew where I was headed without thinking, and I paused in the doorway to the office, my fingers curling into the worn wood of the doorframe.

I'd come here to fix this. If I couldn't do that with Wilder, I'd find another way.

The nice laptop I'd ordered for ranch use last year was gone. In its place was its predecessor, a clunky old machine that took ten minutes to do anything and threw up errors like it was being paid to slowly die.

Had Luke sold the laptop too?

I sat down at the desk and opened the old computer. I logged onto it, not surprised that Luke hadn't bothered to change the password.

While I waited for the email to load, I went digging in the desk drawers. Luke didn't believe in a filing system. I was pretty sure the folders I'd made hadn't had anything new added to them since I'd moved out. Instead, I sorted through piles of papers in the drawers. Receipts, invoices, payroll verifications, employee information.

"A-plus for privacy, Luke," I said as I glanced at a new ranch hand's personal information.

The email account loaded as I closed the first drawer. I hit the down arrow on the keyboard, scanning subject lines as they slowly moved by.

Agreement Signed by All Parties.

"Wait. Wait!" I sighed out loud as the dumb computer kept scrolling, a solid ten seconds behind from when I lifted my finger from the arrow. When it finally stopped, I made my way back up, one line at a time.

The computer chugged along, finally opening the email I wanted as I imagined every creak of the house meant someone was here.

I didn't want to think about what Luke might do if he found me here.

The attachment I clicked finally opened a PDF. I skimmed it, my heart thumping so hard it was almost impossible to hear anything else.

... agree to sell to Lucas Noble for the total sum of ...

...acres located northwest of the boundary line of property owned by

. . .

... deeded to Thomas Harker on ...

This was it.

I couldn't believe it. I'd found proof that the amusement park company agreed to sell Luke acreage that had belonged to the Harkers.

I forwarded the email as fast as I could—in other words, very slowly—to myself, then deleted evidence that I'd forwarded it. Then I logged off the computer and closed it before slipping out the office door.

My footsteps echoed down the hallway. I didn't know what I was going to do with that agreement, but at least I had something useful. Something that could maybe salvage all of this and make up for the enormous mistake I'd made.

I closed the outside door behind me and started to slip the key back into the grill when Wilder appeared out of nowhere.

"Marybeth?"

I slapped a hand over my heart as I closed the lid to the grill. "You scared me."

He glanced at the grill. "What are you doing here?"

"I came to see you."

Wilder pulled off the hat he must've borrowed from Luke. He looked exhausted, with shadows around his eyes and a face wearier than any ranch work could've made it. "What about your shop?"

"I closed it."

That seemed to wake him up. He tilted his head. "What do you mean? What happened?"

I couldn't tell whether he was serious or if he was playing me. And honestly, I was sick of it. "*You* happened. Did you repeat what I told you about Violet to Luke?"

His eyes widened in understanding, and he laid the hat down on top of the grill. "He found a way to use that."

I gaped at him. At least he wasn't trying to deny it. "I thought I was helping you, but all you did was use me. Is the story about Makayla true? Or did you lie about that to earn more sympathy?"

"*What*? You think I'd really make that up?"

"I don't know what to think right now. First Drake, now you. I feel like I can't trust any of you. You showed up here out of nowhere, I helped you, and you took the one moment I let my guard down to get information so Luke could screw over my boyfriend and his family. I was trying to be your sister, Wilder. Your friend. And now . . ." I shook my head, running out of words.

You ruined everything.

"I'm your family, Marybeth. Nothing's going to change that, ever," he said. "But given the circumstances, you can't drop something like that into my lap and not expect me to mention it to Luke. Family comes first. Maybe that's something you've forgotten."

I stared at him. I was still so naïve, and I hated myself for it.

"Unless you want to bring this up with Luke, you might want to head out." Wilder nodded at the sound of a four-wheeler approaching.

Talking to Luke was the last thing I wanted. Without even so much as a "goodbye" to Wilder, I turned on my heel.

But I was only a couple of steps away from the back door when a truck emerged from the trees into the driveway.

Gabe's truck.

Chapter Thirty

Ward

I was halfway out the door of the truck when Gabe grabbed my arm. "Stay here."

"Not a chance."

He eyed me like I was ten and he knew everything. "Do you see her car?"

I didn't, but I made a show of looking anyway. "Doesn't matter. Maybe she stopped by and left." Before he could rebut that idea, I nodded toward where Luke Noble had just parked a four-wheeler. "And I'm not letting you go out there by yourself."

Gabe paused, his eyes finally finding Marybeth, who seemed frozen in place as she looked between Luke and us. "What is she doing here?"

"I'm coming with you."

"Ward—"

"I can keep my cool, remember? I don't *care* if Old Man Noble poisoned some cattle or tore down some fences fifteen years ago." In other words, I wasn't planning to step out of the truck and start throwing punches.

But I would if I had to.

"All right. Fine." I'd worn him down. He let go of me, and we got out of the truck.

"Gabe," Marybeth started toward him, but he moved faster, meeting her before she reached the driveway. I followed behind, my eyes on her brothers.

Luke dropped a few choice words, shoving a cooler into Wilder's hands, before following Marybeth. It didn't escape my notice that he had a pistol strapped to his hip.

"What the hell are you doing here?" His voice echoed off the parked trucks.

Marybeth turned around, acting as a much too tiny wall between her brother and Gabe.

"My brother's looking for his wife," Gabe said. "She been over here?"

Luke shot me a look that could've melted steel. I moved forward slowly, not trusting him to act rationally. "No," he said, his voice short. "What makes you think that? Wilder?" He turned to his brother.

Wilder shook his head.

"There's your answer. If you think she's off looking for someone better, try the bars. Wouldn't be too hard for her find it."

I curled my fingers into my palms. He was goading me, and I wasn't about to fall for it. My mind was an exhausted, ragged mess after that argument with Violet, but I was smarter than that.

As mad as I was at her, I never even thought she'd just pack up and leave. But that was exactly what she'd done. I didn't know why I wanted to find her. But I couldn't let her go without knowing she was okay. So here I was, stepping onto property I had no business coming around, looking for her.

"Come on," Marybeth said to Gabe, placing her hand on his arm. "Let's go."

He looked down at her hand like it was something poisonous.

"Relax," Wilder said to Gabe from where he still stood near the door. "She came out here to give me an earful."

Luke shot a glare at him, and Wilder shrugged.

Luke turned his attention back to us, his hand resting over the pistol. "I already told you to leave."

Marybeth tugged at Gabe's arm, whispering something to him. With one last hard glance at Luke, Gabe relented and began to back away.

But I didn't move.

Whether it was the obnoxious flex with the gun, the fire still raging within at Violet's lack of trust in me, or I'd just finally had enough of losing, I took a step forward instead.

"Ward," Marybeth hissed from somewhere behind me as I kept walking.

Luke pinched the bridge of his nose, like he couldn't handle being bothered with me. "You deaf, Harker?"

"You think you've won." The words came out like spider's silk. Smooth, confident, and deadly.

He smiled. "I *know* I've won. That's what my family does. We win."

I glanced away, feigning boredom before slowly looking back at him. "You know what my family does? We survive. By any means possible. We find the weak point, and then we press until we get what we need."

The words lingered between us. He knew what I meant. We might've been kids, but the only reason Pops survived was because he hadn't been afraid to do exactly that to Carson Noble. He bought the land for a song, took half the illicit business with it, and built a small empire.

And the Nobles had never let us forget it.

"What are you going to do?" He spat the words at me. "Steal half my herd? Break my foreman's legs? Burn a barn?"

"You already did that, from what I heard."

He smirked. "Turnabout, and all that. Besides, like I said, we already won. Prison, remember?"

"That was only a battle, Noble. This is a war, and you're not winning."

The smirk turned into a smile, and Luke raised his arms out to the sides. "Except I am. Your wife ran off with her tail between her legs. She doesn't care about you or this town. It won't be long now before her company gives up. That land will *never* be a ranch again. And it'll never be yours."

"Wait and see," I said, pretending as if his words about Violet didn't gut me. "We're bringing you down. Right back into the dirt, where you belong. Because as long as I live, I'm going to make sure everyone knows the truth about your family. You're just as dirty as we are."

He gave a short laugh, and then threw up a hand toward Gabe's truck. "Get out of here, Harker. You come back again, you'll be leaving in pieces."

I held his gaze a moment before turning away.

I may not have ever cared about the bad blood between our families, but I did now.

When I started a fight in business, I didn't lose. And I wasn't about to start now.

Even if I had to do it alone.

Chapter Thirty-one

Violet

I stared up at the textured ceiling from the guest bed at Mom and Dad's house. This wasn't the home I grew up in. They sold that before Dad got diagnosed, thinking they'd downsize and live out their best retirement dreams.

Someone shuffled down the hallway. It was probably Mom. She didn't sleep much, worrying about Dad and finances and every other terrible thing that came along with cancer.

I turned over and faced the empty side of the bed. It was weird, sleeping alone after getting used to having someone else beside me. Or two someones really, if I included Barker. I stretched a hand across the bed, like that would magically erase everything that had happened and make Ward appear.

He hadn't called. He hadn't even texted. I supposed some part of me hoped that when he came back to the room at the B&B and found me and my stuff gone, he'd come running after me.

But why should he? I was the one who'd kept things from him.

I sighed and sat up in bed. I wasn't falling back asleep now. Outside the door, Mom moved down the hallway again.

I knew why I hadn't told Ward about Dad or about the money or the way Chestnut Moon held my job and my parents' house over me. I didn't want his pity—and I definitely didn't want him trying to help out with a problem that wasn't his.

But now I wasn't so sure. Would it have been pity? Or something more?

I buried my head in my hands and muffled a silent scream. I'd never been in a situation—in a relationship, I suppose—like this. I'd had boyfriends, but nothing serious. Nothing long-term. They were fun flings, and they ended when one of us got bored.

It was different with Ward, and I didn't even realize it was happening until it did. And then I'd found myself in the garden at the B&B telling him all the reasons I liked him. He hadn't run away. He hadn't gotten bored.

Our fake marriage had started to turn into something real.

But I didn't know how to do *real*, and now Ward didn't trust me, and I was going to lose my job if I didn't figure out something fast.

I'd been home for two days, and I'd managed to pack up my apartment but I hadn't reached out at all to Mac. And tonight was the town meeting in Bent Creek. He'd probably call me later, ready to hear what I had planned to put everything back into order. I picked up my phone now, ready to type out a text promising that I was on it, but the words wouldn't come.

I wasn't on it. I had no idea at all what to do. And Mac was the last person I wanted to talk to right now.

And if I was being honest, my job was the last thing I cared about.

A knock came at my door, and Mom opened it just slightly.

"I'm awake," I said, laying my phone down.

She sat on the edge of my bed, like I was a little girl sick with a fever who needed comforting. I wasn't sick, but I could definitely use some comforting.

"Did you get everything packed?" she asked.

"Yeah. The movers are coming today. I hope there's enough room in the garage for it."

"If not, we can put some things in the basement," Mom said. She'd refused to let me get a storage unit, instead moving both her and Dad's cars out of their garage to make room for my things. "I still hate that you're giving up your apartment."

"I don't mind." And I didn't, not if that money could help them. It would mean I wouldn't have to go back to Chestnut Moon for more help, and something about that made everything feel much better.

She reached out and smoothed a strand of my hair. "Do you want to share why you came back so suddenly?"

I chewed on my lip. I'd shown up here without notice and then made myself so busy that I'd barely seen her. Now that what I'd had with Ward was over, I supposed I should say something.

Almost over, a voice in my head reminded me. I still had to get a divorce.

That thought felt like a knife slicing through my heart, and I shoved it aside. Instead, I opened my mouth, and the entire story poured out. To Mom's credit, she kept her shocked look to a minimum, reaching for my hand as I wound to the end of the story.

"And that's it," I said, shrugging as if it didn't feel like my entire world was crumbling apart.

"That doesn't sound like *it*," she said. "You left, and . . ."

I shrugged again. "I haven't heard anything from him."

"Hmm." She nodded and looked down at our hands. "Do you miss him?"

It was a simple question, and yet it felt like the hardest thing to answer. Tears pricked at my eyes. I swallowed hard. I couldn't lie to her—or to myself. So I nodded.

"Does he know that?"

"I don't know," I whispered. "It doesn't matter. He doesn't trust me."

"Violet."

I looked up at her. And suddenly, all I wanted was for her to wrap her arms around me and tell me it was all going to be okay. She read my mind and did just that.

And finally, I let myself cry.

Mom said nothing for a while, not until I'd let all the tears fall that I'd held back. When I finally pulled away and swiped at my face with the back of my hand, she reached for a tissue, held it out, and said, "Do you want some advice?"

I nodded. I was so lost.

"Okay. First, relationships aren't easy."

I let out a laugh as I balled the tissue in my hand. "I figured that one out."

She smiled. "Good. If you want this to have a chance at working out, you need to be honest with him. You can't have something serious with a man and keep parts of yourself hidden. Same goes for him, by the way."

I grimaced. "I don't think he has that problem. He's told me everything." I knew about his shady family past, his ex-girlfriend, why he lost his job. He didn't spare me from anything ugly; he put it all out there.

It was me who had failed him.

"You can tell him now. No one is perfect," Mom said. "And if someone expects that from you, they aren't your person."

"How did you get so good at this? *You're* perfect."

She laughed. "Not by any stretch of the imagination, kiddo. Now, are you planning to meet those movers today?"

I stared at her. "You can't drop something like that and *not* tell me what you mean."

"That's a story for another time," Mom said with an enigmatic smile. "The movers?"

"Um . . ." I tried to imagine myself at the apartment, supervising a bunch of college guys carrying out my couch and my kitchen table.

And I just . . . couldn't.

It wasn't where I needed to be. Not today.

Not even fully comprehending what I was doing, I reached for my phone, ready to call and reschedule the movers.

Mom rested her hand on mine. "I'll go. You take care of what you need to. I can make sure everything gets here."

"You can't do that. Dad—"

"Livvy is coming over later with the kids. She can keep him company."

"Are you sure? I don't have to move today."

Mom patted my hand. "Entirely sure. You'd better get dressed and come eat these pancakes I made. It's a few hours' drive down to Bent Creek, isn't it?"

I smiled at her as something like hope crept into my heart. I might not be able to salvage the ranch land, but maybe there was still a chance for me and Ward.

Mom slipped out the door. I got dressed, threw a few things into a bag, and grabbed my phone to type out a quick text.

I'm okay. I'm sorry if I made you worry. I'll explain everything soon. I hesitated for just a moment, doubts creeping in. Did he even care if I was okay? Had he worried at all? Would he give me the time of day?

I had nothing to lose now.

So I hit send, grabbed my bag, and met Mom in the kitchen.

Chapter Thirty-two

Ward

The town still hadn't stopped talking.

I slipped into the back of the town hall, flanked by my brothers and their girlfriends. One by one, people eyed us from their seats.

I thought back to what Mrs. Garcia had said, that day on Main Street when I told her all about plans I'd never even considered real before they'd come out of my mouth. She'd told me that she was glad we'd turned out all right. That the Harker boys weren't all bad, despite everything we'd grown up with.

I'd believed it. People smiled at me, talked to me, asked me about my younger brothers Mav and Colt, told me they were glad to see me, bragged on how Nick had helped fix up a park bench and how Jackson worked so hard up at the resort.

And now all of that had gone up in flames. The looks we got now as we found seats in an empty row in the middle of the room were suspicious. It sent me right back to high school, to that day when everyone found out Pops had been arrested.

All that work my brothers had put into becoming a part of this town, building the Harker name into something more than drugs and prison, and I'd shown up and managed to ruin it over the course of a few weeks.

As good as I thought I was with people, I'd completely misread Violet.

I pulled out my phone to distract myself from the glances that kept coming our way. And right there, at the top of my text messages, was the one Violet had sent earlier.

I'm okay. I'm sorry if I made you worry. I'll explain everything soon.

What the hell did that mean? When was *soon*? And was me worrying that she'd run off and gotten murdered the only thing she was sorry for?

I swallowed an irritated sigh and clicked off my phone.

"She finally texted?" Gabe asked. Marybeth sat next to him, her mind clearly elsewhere as Larkin chatted with Emily.

"Yeah," I said, realizing too late that he'd read the message over my shoulder. "It doesn't mean anything."

"If she calls, it's worth hearing her out though, right?"

I shrugged. "Maybe." I wasn't sure if that would help or make me feel even worse. She'd taken me for a fool, but beyond that, I'd thought we'd had something. I put myself out there, after Parker had ripped me apart, just like some family-run business oblivious to the giant corporation ready to gobble me up.

Violet and Chestnut Moon had done exactly that. And I'd missed the signs by a mile.

"Are you going to say something?" I nodded toward the front of the room, where the council members had taken their seats.

"Yeah. I don't know what it'll do, but we're not going down without a fight," Gabe said.

"I'm sorry. I messed this up pretty bad."

"You didn't. You did what you could. It looked good for a while, didn't it?"

"I suppose." It was hard to admit out loud that we'd almost succeeded. That *I'd* almost succeeded.

As the mayor called the meeting to order, I thought about what I was going to do next. Go back to LA, even though the thought of the traffic, the perfect-on-the-outside people, and my sleek, empty apartment left me feeling cold. I'd have to find another job, which I dreaded for some reason. I had Barker, at least. Maybe that would help. Staying here was out of the question now, not when every inch of this town made me think of Violet. And when everyone thought that all I cared about was money.

The door behind us creaked just slightly. I turned around out of habit, along with half the room.

Violet slipped inside.

My heart thudded to a stop. She looked different, and it took me a couple of seconds to figure out why.

She was in jeans and a sweatshirt. It was a far cry from the put-together outfit she'd worn at the last town meeting. She looked more like the Violet I'd seen relaxing at night in our room at the B&B, or the one who'd taken Barker for walks.

She looked like *my* Violet.

Stop it. I clenched my jaw and dug my nails into my palms. She wasn't mine. We had a piece of paper that told the world we were together, but we weren't. Not really. And I wasn't going to fool myself again.

I forced myself to turn around, even though I could almost feel her moving up the aisle and slipping into the row opposite us.

The mayor had finished speaking, and I'd missed every word she'd said. The man from the amusement park company was talking now, painting rainbows and bunnies and freaking unicorns dancing through the streets, and everyone was nodding, eating it up.

Luke Noble sat in the front row in the section opposite us, next to his brother. I could just make out the satisfied smirk on his face. His arms were crossed, and he looked like he'd just been crowned king of Bent Creek.

I'd promised him he wouldn't win. That we'd be bringing him down. That pledge was like fire through my veins. I still didn't know how it would happen, but I'd figure it out, even from LA. Maybe that would make going back less painful, if I had a vendetta to work toward.

Violet had given up on me, but I wasn't giving up on my family.

Luke must've felt me staring at him, because he turned just slightly and met my eyes. I smiled, fully aware I probably appeared insane. He simply looked amused.

I sat back, and Gabe nudged me with his elbow. "I've got enough on my plate, keeping those two in line." He nodded at Nick and Jackson. "Don't make me need to look after you too."

"I'm good. I handle all my revenge on paper."

Gabe watched me a moment, like he didn't quite believe me. Only the mayor calling for any other remarks made him look away.

He was halfway to standing when Marybeth shot up instead.

"Me," she said. "I have something to say."

Gabe gaped at her, clearly at a loss for words.

She was out of her seat and on her way up front before he could say anything.

Chapter Thirty-three

Marybeth

Hundreds of eyes stared at me.

I almost lost my nerve, right then and there. The printed-out pages crinkled in my pocket as I shifted my weight from one foot to the other.

"Go ahead." Samantha Farrow, who was sitting to the right of the podium, nodded and smiled at me.

I gripped the edges of the podium and forced a smile back. "Thanks." I looked back out at everyone, my eyes finally landing on Gabe.

This was for him. For him and his brothers. I'd messed up, but I was making up for it now.

"Hello." My voice echoed in the speakers, and I almost jumped backward at the sound of it. "I'm Marybeth Noble, if you don't know me. I own Bent Creek Christmas."

Everyone knew that. This was a room mostly filled with my teachers, friends of my parents, people I'd gone to school with. I didn't know why I was introducing myself, except that it was something easy to say. Several people smiled at me, but most just watched me with curiosity.

"I'm Luke's sister." Another thing everyone knew. Luke was right in the front row, Wilder next to him, and my gaze caught his. He was sitting up straight, but he wasn't smiling.

It was like he knew what was coming.

I swallowed the massive amount of fear that fluttered in my stomach and looked down at the podium. Once I did this, there was no going back.

But if I didn't, there would be no going forward. Gabe wasn't angry with me, but he was careful. I could see it in the way he spoke, and the way he left the room to take calls now.

Luke had once told me that I had to make a choice. I thought he was being ridiculous, issuing an ultimatum like that.

But he was right.

"I know you've all heard the rumors," I said into the microphone, averting my gaze from Luke. "About Chestnut Moon. About Ward Harker and Violet Barnes. Gabe was going to get up here tonight and tell you that none of it is true. That only Ward and Violet can speak to their feelings, that their marriage is really no one's business but their own, although it's clear to all of us that they're crazy in love with each other. That he and his brothers want that land back more than anything. That they want to be—they *are*—part of this town, and they want to preserve the heritage of that ranch and bring it back to life. All of that is true. And that the accusations made against Ward and Violet—that they're only in it for the money—couldn't be more wrong."

I paused, glancing at Gabe again as people quietly whispered to each other. He gave me a little smile and nodded. And suddenly I felt so much braver. I might have been on the verge of losing one family, but I'd already gained another.

I pressed my hands against the podium to steady myself before I continued. "Gabe had no idea I was getting up here tonight. I'm sure he's still wondering why I did. But it's because I have more to say than what I just told you."

I took a deep breath and dipped shaking fingers into my pocket. The papers crinkled loudly as I pulled them out.

"This is a copy of an agreement between Mr. Larson's company, Interstate Amusements, and my brother, Luke Noble," I heard myself saying. "The only ulterior motive for anything that's happened recently is in this agreement." I held it up a little higher, my hand trembling as Luke jumped up from his seat.

"Mr. Noble," Mayor Barry said warily. "Sit down. You'll have your turn in a moment."

Luke scowled at me, and Wilder yanked him back down.

It was enough to make me want to shut up and run back to my chair—but I forced myself to stay put. This wasn't for me. This was for Gabe. It was for Ward and Violet.

"This is an agreement promising the sale of several acres of land on the old Harker ranch from Interstate Amusements to Luke, once the sale of the land from the county is finalized. I checked the old deeds at the courthouse, and these are the same parcels of land that my dad sold to Tom Harker almost twenty years ago during the drought."

The room erupted into conversation. Snatches of it reached my ears.

"He's only in this to get land for himself."

"Pulling one over on us."

"I never would've thought he'd do that."

I felt like I'd run a marathon. Completely out of breath, I slowly lowered the agreement to the podium. Gabe's look of surprise turned to an enormous grin as Ward clapped him on the shoulder. And Violet . . . her mouth hung open. She closed it when she caught me looking at her, and then mouthed *thank you*.

"You sneaky little . . ." Luke stood just in front of the podium as the room buzzed. He was furious—it rolled off him in waves.

I knew exactly what I was doing. I'd done it, and now I had to deal with the fallout.

He shook his head. "That day you came over. You went through my computer. I swear, Marybeth. Did he know?" He didn't have to point to Gabe for me to know who he was talking about. "Did he put you up to it?"

"He didn't." I felt strangely calm, now that everything was out in the open. "You once told me to choose a side, Luke. I guess I finally did."

Wilder closed in, glancing between the two of us, as Luke watched me with the kind of hard look I'd only ever seen my father give someone who had gotten on his bad side.

"I thought I could save you if I cut you out. But I can't. I'm done, Marybeth. Don't step foot on my property again," he said in a flat voice. "Don't call our parents. Don't ask Wilder for help. Don't—" He cut himself off with an angry shake of his head.

"Come on. This is over," Wilder said as Mayor Barry tried unsuccessfully to call everyone back to their seats.

And just before Luke tore his eyes from me, I saw something in his gaze I hadn't seen in a long time.

Sadness.

I took a step forward, but Wilder held up his hand.

"You've done enough," he said.

And then he turned and followed Luke into the crowd. I dropped my arms to my sides as I let out a shuddering breath.

I was alone.

"Marybeth." Gabe appeared where my brothers had been. He took one look at me and wrapped his arms around me. "It's okay. I've got you."

Somehow, without witnessing what had just happened, he knew. I let go of myself and leaned against him, my hands wrapping around his shoulders as tears leaked from my eyes. "I don't have a family anymore," I said, my voice barely a whisper.

"Yes, you do," Larkin said. She was standing right next to us with Nick, who nodded in agreement.

I turned my head, leaning just far enough away from Gabe that I could see them all. Larkin and Nick. Jackson and Emily. And there, on the fringes, Ward.

My heart might have been in pieces, but they were there to pick all the shards up for me. I gave them a weak smile. "Thank you."

"We should be thanking you," Jackson said.

I shook my head, holding on tightly to Gabe. Over Jackson's shoulder, another familiar face appeared.

Violet.

Jackson turned and spotted her. "Let's go talk to the mayor. See what happens next." He gave a pointed look to Ward.

Meanwhile, I caught Violet's eye. *Good luck*, I mouthed to her.

I didn't think she needed it, though. Not with the look I saw on Ward's face as we walked away.

Chapter Thirty-four

Ward

"H i."

The word lingered in the air between us. I should've been angry, but that was gone.

The only thing I felt right now was relief.

I lifted a hand and gestured toward the door. "Outside?"

Violet nodded, clearly eager to get away from all these people. I led the way, glancing back a couple of times to make sure she hadn't gotten pulled aside in the crowd. People wanted to say something, to talk to us. I could feel them moving toward me as I pushed my way through. But I kept my head down until I'd rounded the side of the building and found my way to the narrow alley in the back.

We could still hear voices from around the front, but no one was back here, not at this hour of the evening. I gestured at a giant stone that sat in between the town hall property and the ice cream parlor next door.

Violet sat, facing the alley. I hesitated a moment, then I sat too. The boulder was big enough to allow for a few inches between us, and that was what I needed right now.

"You came back," I said, careful to keep the emotion from my voice as I looked up, over the top of the building across the alley to where, in the daylight, you could see the peaks of the mountains.

She clasped her hands around her knees. "I shouldn't have run. I'm sorry, Ward. For that. And everything."

Her voice broke a little. I pressed my fingers against the stone. It would be so easy to reach out to her, to take her hand and pretend nothing had happened.

But it had. And I refused to be the man Parker had discarded ever again. I deserved better than that.

"Where did you go?" I asked.

A beat passed, then another. I repressed a sigh. She wasn't going to tell me. It would be another closely-guarded secret she didn't trust me with.

"My parents' house," she said, jerking me out of my thought spiral. She turned then, facing me with her knees just barely grazing my leg. "I went there because it's the only place I thought I'd feel like I could be myself. Mom, Dad, my sister Livvy—they're the only people who have ever really had my back. I don't have close friends. I've never had a real relationship. I have my family and my job, and that's it. Well—" She gave a short laugh. "I *did* have a job. Maybe I still do after what happened in there. But, you know what?"

I stared at her. "What?" I said cautiously.

"I don't think I want it anymore. My job, I mean." She shook her head. "I've never said that out loud, but I've been thinking it for a while. I *don't* like my job. I don't like my boss, or the board. I don't like that they helped me and then held it over my head. What kind of people do that?"

"Corporate types," I said wryly.

She laughed a little. "You're right. I don't think I like any of them anymore. I don't want to *be* them anymore. You know that one time I had to talk the sweetest little old couple into selling their property to me? It was all they had. Generations of that family had lived on that land, and guess who owns it now?"

I didn't have to guess.

"I *hated* that. I hated the way it made me feel afterward. But I was good at it, and they gave me more important work, and then when my dad got sick, they helped me. Yes, Dad is sick. He has a cancer I can barely pronounce, much less understand, and he's exhausted and weak. My parents took out a mortgage on their house—which they'd paid for in full after selling the old one a few years ago—just to afford his bills. But that wasn't enough, and so it's up to me and Livvy. Except she has no money, so really, it's on me. I pay the utilities and the mortgage and the medical bills. It's so bad, I had to give up my apartment and move everything into their garage. I didn't want to take more money from the company. They paid three years' worth of back taxes, and they told me that if I didn't do what they said and marry you, they'd file a lien. So Luke was right about one thing. I *am* broke. I mean, I have an income, but every single penny of it is pretty much spent before I get it."

She was talking as if she'd never shared a word of this with anyone. "Vi—"

"Please, Ward. Let me finish. I didn't tell you all of this because I didn't want you think I was weak. That I was some damsel who needed saving. I didn't want your money. And I *really* didn't want your pity. So I kept it to myself, which is what I've always done. I've never had anyone ask me anything more than, 'What do you want for lunch?' or 'Can you lend me twenty bucks?' Guys, I mean. I'm talking about guys. Well, girls too, I guess. I took a huge chance telling Marybeth about my dad. I barely said much of anything, and look what happened there."

"She feels really bad about that. She said it wasn't on purpose."

Violet nodded, her teeth finding her bottom lip again. "I kind of hoped so, after what she did tonight."

I took a deep breath, and her eyes, almost black in the one street light overhead, found me again. I was ready to get to the point. "Why are you telling me all of this?"

She twisted her hands together. "I got some really good advice. If I want a real relationship, I have to let the other person in. To every part of my life, even the not-so-good parts. I can't just keep everything to myself."

That tiny spark of hope lit inside me at her words. "Am I that other person?"

She smiled a little. "Yes. I think you are. If you want to be. Although I understand if it's too late—"

"Do you trust me?" It was the most important question of all.

She didn't hesitate to answer. "Entirely. I—"

I didn't let her finish. Instead, I placed a hand on either side of her face and kissed her as if she'd been gone for months instead of days.

"Ward," she said, pulling away just slightly. "Does that mean you forgive me?"

"What do you think?" I grinned at her before capturing her lips with mine again.

"Ward?" She pulled away again. "Does that mean you don't want a divorce from our fake marriage?"

I let my body answer that question, crushing her to me with the intention of never letting her go again.

"Ward?" she said again after a few minutes, when she'd found her way onto my lap.

I let out a growl this time. "I love you. Don't you dare divorce me. Yes, you can have a real wedding. Now stop asking me questions."

She dissolved into laughter until I caught her mouth with mine.

"I love you too," she whispered against my lips when we finally came up for air.

As she wound her fingers through my hair, I knew I was never going back to LA.

I was home.

Chapter Thirty-five

Violet

Two months later...

The barn had been transformed.

When we'd walked through it weeks ago in the hopes of becoming the Petersons' first wedding customers, it had still needed a ton of work. Now it was decorated simply in greenery with white tulle and haybales for seating.

"Violet? Is everything okay?" Marybeth stood beside me in her pale pink dress, searching the barn and all the people in it for something wrong.

"It's *perfect*," I said, breathing the word out.

"Oh, thank goodness." She placed a hand against her chest before turning to me. "You look gorgeous, by the way."

I smoothed down the front of my dress. It wasn't anything fancy. Just a simple white sheath dress with some beading at the top and the hem, but it was everything I'd ever wanted. Much better than the first time around. "Thank you."

"Larkin's ready. I think it's almost time to start." Marybeth tugged my arm to pull me back to where the others waited.

But I paused for just a second. I wanted to get a look at Ward, waiting for me up front. The second he spotted me from where he stood next to Nick, I waved.

"Seriously, Violet. Don't you know it's bad luck for him to see you in your dress before the wedding?"

"We're already married, remember? I don't think that matters in this situation." But I let her lead me back to where everyone else was waiting.

Larkin looked perfect in her off-white, floor-length lace dress, with her hair falling in soft waves around her face. "Can you believe we're doing this?" she said.

"Thank you for letting us tag along on your wedding," I replied. The double wedding had been all Larkin's idea, after she'd heard that Ward and I wanted to have a real ceremony.

"I should be thanking you. This is way less terrifying with a friend." She squeezed my hand.

"It's time!" Livvy ran over to me and smoothed down my hair, which I had pulled back in a chignon. "Dad, are you ready?"

He nodded from the wheelchair that Mom would push him in. My heart lit up, seeing him here. It meant the world to me that my dad would walk me down the aisle.

The kids went first—Larkin's son Diego as the ring bearer, and Livvy's twins as flower girls. Marybeth winked at me as Gabe took her arm. They followed Emily and Jackson down the aisle, and Livvy and her husband went soon after. The bridesmaids and groomsmen in place, the strings began to play a more traditional tune. Larkin shot me a nervous grin, and then began to walk down the aisle with her mother escorting her.

And then it was my turn. With Mom and Dad at my side, I couldn't keep the smile off my face as what felt like the entire town watched me make my way to Ward.

I leaned down so Dad could give me a kiss on the cheek. Mom hugged me, and then Ward took my hands.

I glanced at Larkin as the ceremony began. She gazed up at Nick, and I wasn't sure I'd ever seen two people more in love. She'd told me their entire story, and I loved that happy endings like theirs existed in the world. It gave me hope—for Dad, for the ranch that Chestnut Moon still owned after the town's vehement disapproval of the county's condemnation action, and for the wide-open future that lay in front of Ward and me. I'd quit my job a month ago, and had already accepted a remote position researching titles and deeds for another investment company. It would require some travel, but we could go anywhere—including Missoula, where Ward had a lead on a great position. We could be near my parents, and close enough to Bent Creek that Ward could help his brothers. They were more determined than ever to get their ranch back. Eventually, we hoped to move back here.

Ward held my hands tightly in his, his eyes never leaving me as he repeated his vows. I barely heard myself say the same words, even though I wanted to remember every moment of today.

Nick and Larkin promised eternity to each other, and before I knew it, the minister was pronouncing us each man and wife. Before he could even get the instructions to kiss the bride out of his mouth, Ward had swooped down, gathered me in his arms, and claimed my lips.

Laughter echoed through the barn. Music started up again, and Ward finally leaned back, his eyes glowing.

"I think this means you're stuck with me," he said.

"I already was," I reminded him. "But I don't mind."

He dropped a kiss on my nose as we turned to walk back down the aisle. Larkin came up alongside me and took my hand, and the four of us strode down the aisle together.

Family, I decided, was an unbreakable bond—whether you were born into it, married into it, or simply found it.

I'd finally found the people I could trust, and I knew they'd be there for me when I needed them.

Ward wrapped an arm around my shoulder as we reached the end of the aisle, and I leaned into his embrace, reaching up to wrap my arms around his neck.

"I love you forever," I whispered.

"Forever," he repeated, before kissing me again.

Epilogue

Colton

They were lucky it wasn't raining.

I stood at the edge of the reception, sipping bland beer and hoping no one noticed that I'd missed the ceremony.

My brothers were dancing with their brides. It was crazy to see them married. And from the looks of it, Gabe and Jackson wouldn't be too far behind. I hadn't told any of them I was here yet. They didn't even know I was coming.

For that matter, *I* didn't know I was coming until this morning. Not until I'd gotten a cryptic message from Samantha yesterday.

I messed up so bad. I don't know what to do.

And that was it. No replies, no answers to my calls. I could've asked Jackson to check on her, but then he'd want to know why, and no way was I explaining that. Especially when he had best man duties to deal with today.

So I did what anyone would do when the best friend they'd ever had in their life says something distressing and then disappears. I got on a plane, came back to Bent Creek, and made an appearance at the wedding my brothers had invited me to.

I was hoping she'd be here, and I was right. She was dancing with some guy I'd never seen before, laughing and looking up at him like he'd promised her the world.

I threw back the rest of the beer and set the glass on a nearby table. I'd run all the way here for what?

To see the girl I still thought about every day in the arms of some other guy.

And to make it worse, my brothers looked so happy. They were all paired up, and while I was glad for them, it brought home the fact that I was alone, pining after someone I only talked to in texts these days.

I shouldn't have come here. This place was full of ghosts. I'd just graduated middle school when we left. Kicked out of the only home I'd ever had and sent with my brothers to live with an aunt in Livingston.

Sam and I had sent emails back then. Keeping in touch even after she said her parents told her not to. They were right, given how I'd turned out. We graduated to texts later, after I got myself a phone. I hadn't seen her in person since the day I left Bent Creek.

But there she was, just as pretty as ever. And happy.

I should leave her alone.

I turned around, deciding I'd stop by to see my brothers tomorrow before I left. Tell Nick and Ward congratulations. Tell Gabe I was sorry I wasn't much help with their efforts to reclaim the ranch. Let them know I was glad the county had given up on turning the land into an amusement park.

I was halfway back to the car I'd borrowed when a hand clapped my shoulder. I shot around, ready to land a punch, but it was only Gabe.

He held up a hand. "Hey, Colt, sorry. Didn't mean to scare you. I didn't know you were coming."

"I didn't either," I said, fishing the keys from my pocket.

"Were you leaving?" he asked, looking incredulous.

"Uh . . ." I glanced at the keys, feeling like a jerk. "Don't feel too great. I thought I'd crash at a hotel out by the highway."

"You can stay at our place. Marybeth and I have an extra room."

I nodded, unable how to figure out how to say no. I didn't know if I wanted to anyway. I was running low on cash, and I wasn't sure how long I'd be able to hang on to this car. "Sure, all right. Thanks."

"Here." He pulled a keychain from his pocket and detached a small gold key. "Give me your phone and I'll put in the address."

I handed over my phone and let him enter the address into the maps app. I couldn't see Sam from here. I wondered if she was still dancing with that guy. He had that cocky look, like he'd toss her aside for the next girl in a heartbeat. Was she seeing him? Or was it just casual?

And why the hell had she sent me that text?

Gabe handed me back my phone. "You sure you don't feel up to staying a little longer?"

I shook my head. I didn't hate myself enough to watch Sam leave with someone else. "Tell Nick and Ward congratulations for me. I'll find them tomorrow."

"All right." Gabe slapped my back. "Make yourself at home."

I held up the key. "Got it."

Gabe waved, and I started walking again. I wouldn't stay long tomorrow. Enough time to see my brothers, and then I'd bolt. If Sam wanted help, she knew where to reach me.

I rounded the corner of the barn to where the cars were parked in a field. I pulled out my phone, studying the pin in the map Gabe had left. He lived right in the middle of town on Custer Street. Shouldn't be too hard to find.

I'd just shoved the phone back into my pocket when a flashlight blinded me. I threw up a hand, blinking and looking away.

"This your car?" a voice asked.

Crap. I hadn't been paying attention. I glanced behind me, calculating the odds of success if I ran.

Zero. I'd left my wallet in the car. Rookie mistake.

"Who's asking?" I said, trying to buy time.

The light lowered just enough for my vision to clear. Two Bent Creek police officers stood in front of me, their cruiser parked right behind the car I'd driven here from the airport. I recognized the older one. He squinted at me, like he was trying to place me.

"Answer the question," he said, his words clipped. Scott, that was his name. He came to our door often enough when I was a kid that he was impossible for me to forget.

"Not mine. I borrowed it." I looked from him to the car, like we were just having a regular old conversation.

"That's not what this report we have says," the other cop said.

"Really?" I feigned surprise, even though what I'd said to them was absolutely true. If you looked at it the right way, that was.

"It's stolen," Scott said.

I laughed. "I didn't steal it. Swear to you. I had permission to borrow it."

"Who'd you borrow it from?" Scott asked.

"A new friend."

"Name?"

"Mmm . . ." It started with a T. I'd been so focused on Sam that I'd barely paid attention. "Terry. Yeah, Terry, that's it."

The two cops looked at each other, and I knew right then I was not going to be spending the night in Gabe's spare room.

Thank you so much for reading! I hope you enjoyed Violet and Ward's story. **Find out what happens next** to Colt, who's come back to Bent Creek to help Samantha Farrow, his best friend—and the woman he's been secretly in love with for years—in *A Best Friend in Bent Creek*. And if you haven't read Gabe and Marybeth's story yet, be sure to check out ***A Bent Creek Christmas***.

A big thank you goes to reader Marilyn B. for suggesting the name Barker for Violet and Ward's dog!

Come home to Bent Creek . . . a small town in Montana where everyone knows everyone, secrets live in the shadows of the mountains, and love is waiting to be found. The Harker Brothers Ranch series tells the stories of six brothers—Gabe, Nick, Jackson, Ward, Colt, and Maverick—as they return with one goal: to get the family ranch back in their hands. Reckoning with their family's past, the Nobles, and each other, each one finds love and home again in their hometown.

Join my email newsletter at catiecahill.com to keep up with everything Bent Creek.

More About Catie Cahill

Visit catiecahill.com for a full list of Catie's books.

About Catie

Catie lives with her family in Kentucky but half her heart is in the Rocky Mountains. Catie loves animals, planning travels, reading, and spending time with her family. Visit her online at catiecahill.com.